# Red Stick Men

For Robert, Colleen, and my parents

AUTHOR'S NOTE: "Red Stick" is a local nickname for Baton Rouge, Louisiana. The name "Baton Rouge" is a French translation of the Native-American *isti huma* (or Anglicized "istrouma"), which was the name given the blood-stained tree trunk used as a tribal boundary. The original red stick was located on Scot's Bluff, now part of the campus of Southern University.

Different versions of these stories have appeared in the following places: "It Pours" in *Louisiana Literature,* "Bonnie Ledet" in *Southern Exposure,* "Free Fall" in *The Nebraska Review* and in a chapbook from Volens Press (created by Eileen Wallace with illustrations by Catherine Fairbairn), "Exterminator" in *Crab Orchard Review,* "Roustabout" in *New England Review,* "The Smell of a Car" in *The Texas Review,* "Hardware Man" in *Shenandoah* and in the anthology *Walking on Water,* and "After the River" in *Black Warrior Review.*

Thanks to my friends, colleagues, teachers, students, and previous editors for their support, encouragement, and advice. Special thanks to Patricia Bjorklund and to my editor and advocate, Moira Crone.

www.upress.state.ms.us

Library of Congress Cataloging-in-Publication Data
Parrish, Tim.
    Red stick men : stories / by Tim Parrish.
        p. cm.
    Contents: It pours—Complicity—Bonnie Ledet—
    Free fall—Exterminator—Roustabout—The smell of a
    car—Hardware man—After the river.
    ISBN 1-57806-263-2 (alk. paper)
    1. Oil industry workers—Louisiana—Baton Rouge—
    Fiction. 2. Baton Rouge (La.)—Social life and customs—
    Fiction. I. Title.

PS3566.A7575 R43 2000
813'.54—dc21

                                                    99-087871

British Library Cataloging-in-Publication Data available

# Red Stick Men

## Stories by Tim Parrish

University Press of Mississippi *Jackson*

# Contents

It Pours     11

Complicity     34

Bonnie Ledet     59

Free Fall     88

Exterminator     111

Roustabout     136

The Smell of a Car     160

Hardware Man     187

After the River     211

Busted flat in Baton Rouge . . .

Kris Kristofferson, "Me and Bobby McGee"

# It Pours

The rain dripped crazy time on our walkway as I watched Mr. Ramos emerge from his house across the street. He tilted his head back to study the sky, ran his hand down his throat and peered into the orange bucket beside his porch, a bucket he called his "flood gauge." After he jotted a figure on a pad, he walked to his garage and carefully uncovered his car, a powder blue, '57 Chevy, folding the tarp from one side to the other, then from front to rear. Even in the shade of the garage, the car's pristine paint gleamed. Our mantle clock read 5:42.

Behind me my mother wrote a letter to my brother, Bob, while the news played on TV. Before Bob had left for Vietnam, my father was the one who always watched the news, but now he never did. My father came into the living room and stood next to me.

"Rain finally let up?" he asked. I nodded. Mr. Ramos slid into the driver's seat. Our mantle clock read 5:44. "This keeps on we're all gon wash away," my father said.

The second hand swept on, reached five forty-five and twelve seconds. That morning Mr. Ramos had driven his oldest son, Tootie, to the parish prison to begin serving time for a marijuana bust, and my father had

told me to wait a day before I went to see my friend
Donny. Donny was nine, two years younger than I was.
He and Tootie were the only brothers I knew separated
by more than the eight years that separated me from
Bob. Now both of our brothers were gone.

The Chevy roared alive. "Jeb, close that door," my
mother said, the thick, green air bringing the noise
inside our living room, but I glanced at the mantle
clock and said, "It ain't gonna be loud in a couple of
seconds." Mr. Ramos's engine idled. He stepped out
of the car and opened the hood.

"Ramos shoulda kept a firm hand on that boy," my
father said. "Shouldn't of let him move out."

"Tootie's Bob's age, Harlan," my mother said.

"Bob didn't move out before he went in the army,
did he? He didn't get mixed up with drugs."

Donny came out of the house and put his hands behind his head the way I'd seen prisoners on TV do. The
day before, Donny had yelled at Tootie for pouring beer
into their father's flood gauge and this was the first time
I had seen him since. He stared toward his father, still
under the hood, then called out, "Daddy," twice, much
louder the second time. Mr. Ramos banged closed the
hood and went back behind the wheel. Our clock's second hand glided past the minute forty-five mark. Mr.
Ramos revved the car one last long time. "Now," I said,
and the engine fell silent. Donny spun, went inside and
slammed the door behind him.

"How'd you know that?" my father asked me.

"It's always two minutes," I said.

"Always? What you mean?"

"He starts it four times a day. You ain't noticed?"

My father rubbed the dark bristles on the side of his face. "Four times a day? What for?" he asked. I shrugged. He glanced at my mother. "If Ramos'd paid attention to that boy the way he does that car, he wouldn't be in jail."

A reporter's frantic voice blurted from the TV. On the screen, soldiers crouched in water behind a dirt wall. "Damnit," my father said. "Why you watch that, Winona? They only show you what they want." My mother ignored him. Every time my father was home during the news, he said the same thing. He frowned at the TV. "I'm going out and clear the drain. Water's starting to back up into the yard."

For the last several days, my father had prodded and picked at the street drain with his shovel, even though it never made the water drain any faster. I followed him out and stood with my bare feet in a cool puddle as he poked at the dark hole. After a minute he gazed toward Mr. Ramos, who was back at the flood gauge. "Ramos ever drive that car?" my father asked. I shook my head. My father stabbed with the shovel several more times. "Your momma thinks that news is gon tell her something. Only gon tell her what it wants." He tossed the shovel away and knelt.

"Daddy, you think Bob gets shot at?" I asked.

He reached into the water and searched as if trying

to catch something. "Bob's on a big base, Jeb. Ain't nobody gets shot there."

••

The following morning after the rain let up, I rode
my bike over to the Ramoses' where Donny was oiling
the chain on his bicycle. "Mine rusted, too," I said. He
didn't look at me. In the garage the Chevy's hood was
raised. "He's here?" I asked.

"I can't go anywhere," Donny said.

"Ain't he gonna get a job this summer?" Mr. Ramos
was a high school math teacher who always worked summer jobs.

"Momma got one. Daddy said he wants to work on
his car. He wants me to go get a fuel pump with him."

"A fuel pump? He never drives it."

Donny's brown eyes met mine. He raised up, lifted
the rear of his bike and gave his pedal a hard push, setting his back tire spinning. Mr. Ramos stuck his head
out of the door.

"Donny, you ready to go?"

Donny lowered the tire so that it scuffed to a stop. "I
ain't going," he said.

Mr. Ramos shifted his black-framed glasses. "Yes you
are. Come in and clean your hands." Donny walked to
the hose at the corner of the house and turned it on.
"How's your family?" Mr. Ramos asked me, using the
formal voice he'd adopted in the last few months.

"They're okay," I said.

"Your brother seeing any fighting?"

1 4

I hesitated, not sure how to answer such a strange question. "He ain't been in any fights."

"That's what I thought." Mr. Ramos pointed at his flood gauge. "You know we got over two inches yesterday? That's over four inches this week. Has your father said anything about how soaked the ground is?"

"He said his tomatoes died."

"The Amite River's already backed up into neighborhoods. Donny, hurry with that." Donny slowly scrubbed his fingers, looking at his father through the tops of his eyes. He turned the faucet up, then aimed the hose into the air, creating a small downpour. "Stop that," Mr. Ramos said. Donny smiled and pointed the nozzle's hard spray into Mr. Ramos's bucket. Mr. Ramos bounded toward him, but Donny toppled the bucket, jumped on his bike and hurried away. "Damn," Mr. Ramos said, "I almost had the whole week." He turned off the water and righted the bucket, then bent and touched his fingers to the wet grass. He pressed his hand to the soggy ground. "Go keep an eye on him," he said to me. "No telling what he could do."

Donny was waiting at the end of the street. "Fuck that bucket," he said, and pedalled off. Large puddles lay in the asphalt street's potholes and on its shoulders and Donny hit as many as he could, his fenderless tire throwing muddy water onto his back. He went through every shallow ditch, and I pedalled hard to match his pace. When he headed into a little bamboo thicket, I knew he was going to Hurricane Creek, the deep drainage ditch

that snaked across the city. My bike bumped over the narrow, rooted path through the shoots and over the wooden bridge, and there sat Donny on his bike, staring at the black water rushing
by only five feet below the canal's lip.

"Jesus, I never seen it so fast," I said.

"And deep," Donny said.

The torrent carried sticks and paper trash. Downstream, a snagged limb created a whirlpool. Donny pedalled toward it, his bike tightroping the edge, and I followed, nervous that the muddy ground might give way and send him in. Near the whirlpool he stopped. I pulled up next to him, plucked mud from my chain, flung it from my fingers, then wiped oil on my sock. "You're flipped," I said. With my tongue I tried to catch a few of the rain drops starting to fall. "I wish we had a bateau."

"We could swim across," Donny said.

"Bullshit. That water's gross anyway."

"I could still do it."

"Your daddy told me to keep you from doing something stupid."

"You think you could?"

I shrugged. Donny toed the ground. "I ain't crazy enough to swim in that shit," he said. We both spat into the water.

"Why you think your daddy does his car like that?" I asked. "You know, starting it and all at the same time?"

"I don't know. Ask him." Donny spat again, arching a

white glob into the swirling water where it circled and
went down.

"Didn't he start after Tootie got busted?" I asked.

"Maybe. Why's your old man keep shovelling the
drain?" Donny pointed. "Look."

An island of debris nearly the width of the canal
floated toward us, a shapeless form defying the speed
of the current. I took a step back as it came on, branch-
es bristling and adorned with pieces of ripped plastic
and cloth hanging like banners. In the midst of the island's tangle, a kitchen chair's legs stuck straight up, a
car tire cut a black arc, and a dead bird's wing fluttered.
Donny and I threw handfuls of mud at it. "Keep it from
the whirlpool," I said, but the mass snagged on the limb
anyway. Donny searched the ground, worked from the
mud a chunk of concrete as big as his head. Together
we lifted it and heaved. The chunk crashed through but
the island closed its own hole and went on slowly turning. We gathered rocks and moved to the edge of the
ditch hurling at the thing. Donny slipped, his feet flying
from under him, but he scrambled up and threw again,
moving as close as he could to the water. He cursed at
it, flinging rocks, and I was reaching to grab his shirt,
sure he was about to leap out toward the island, when
it broke away and moved off.

"Let's split," I said. The rain was getting harder, large
drops exploding on my head. I mounted my bike and
turned around, but Donny stood and stared into the
water. "Donny!" I yelled, but he didn't respond. Instead

he took another step down the bank, the mud sliding beneath him until his feet were almost in the water. He turned and pinched his nose, held a hand in the air.

••

The rain kept on, not just a thundershower an afternoon like most summers, but often all day until the water never drained from the edges of our street. The ground squished and oozed beneath my feet, trees drooped under the weight of water, mosquitoes swarmed and the air grew greener as if the plants and rain had mixed to form a hovering stew. In the gulf a tropical depression formed and broke apart. My mother watched it so closely I almost believed her eyes made it dissipate. I began to wake up at 5:45 a.m., to stay awake until 11:45 p.m., in order to hear Mr. Ramos start his Chevy. If I missed it, I felt irritable, especially if I hadn't received a letter or cassette from Bob. Once my whole day was ruined because Bob's letter was soaked so badly that the ink had run.

One evening Brother Thomas, the preacher of our Baptist church, arrived unexpectedly at our house. He had only been our pastor a year and was boisterous and irreverent and theologically contentious in ways that made my father mad, but that night he was solemn as he took a seat in the living room. "Bob's been sending me tapes," Brother Thomas said, and smoothed a hand over his bald head. "He said not to let you all hear what's on them. Still, I think you should have a listen."

My father looked at my mother. "If Bob said not to listen, I don't think we ought to."

"I want to hear," she said. "Jeb, get the cassette player."

When I came back in, my father was standing with his arms crossed, looking sideways at Brother Thomas. "Bob didn't send us this for a reason," my father said. "We best respect that."

My mother took the player from me and inserted the tape. "If you don't want to hear it, Harlan, just leave the room."

"You think you old enough to hear this?" my father asked me.

"Yes, sir," I said.

"You ain't gon like it," my father said. He went to the picture window and stared into the night.

I barely recognized Bob's voice, so halting and without energy. He told in detail about his job, not only how he drove wounded and dead from the helipads and landing field, but also how he bagged body parts and corpses, how their weight made them seem filled with sand. A particular incident, though, an accident, had spurred him to send this tape. A sergeant, who Bob said was the closest thing he had to a father over there, had been checking a rocket tube on a grounded helicopter when the pilot pushed the wrong button. The rocket disintegrated the sergeant's head, then careened through offices and hootches, not exploding but fragmenting, each piece hurtling on, until one struck the

arm of a friend of Bob's who was getting up from sleeping late. Bob had been the first to come on him, had
put out the fire burning in the man's flesh, then helped
carry him to surgery. The man had lost his arm.

"You can't say why shit happens here," Bob said.
"Everybody's scared or wasted or totally whacked just trying to get through. I try to be brave, you know, but I stay
stoned half the time. I want to prove I did right to join,
prove I'm brave, but I got no idea what brave is. I'm
barely keeping it together."

When the tape ended, my father hit the eject button,
removed the cassette and placed it in his pocket. My
mother said my father's name, but my father levelled
his eyes on Brother Thomas.

"You best leave," my father said.

The preacher's head colored pink. "I thought you all
should know."

"If Bob would've wanted his mother to hear this, he
would've sent it to our house. I'd appreciate you not
telling anybody about this, especially not in a sermon."
The preacher nodded. "That son of a bitch," my father
said when the preacher was gone. "Ain't got a lick of
sense."

"I'm glad I heard," my mother said. "We need to
know."

"I already knew," my father said. "I tried to tell him
before he signed up."

"You did not. You never told him."

"I tried. He wouldn't listen. He was set on going. Now he's got to face it like a man."

"A man. He's just a boy." My mother spun and headed to their bedroom. I heard her start crying behind the closed door. My father frowned.

"You don't say nothing about that tape to nobody," he said to me. "I won't have Bob's secrets spread." He walked past me, through the kitchen and into the garage. Through the picture window, I saw him head toward the drain. He jabbed the shovel into the dark slit a couple of times, then reached into his pocket. He flicked the tape down the hole.

••

The following afternoon, my father called Donny and me to the trunk of his car. "Y'all help me unload this," he said, and started handing us brushes, buckets, and jugs that smelled like a swimming pool. "We gon scrub the mildew off the house. Line them jugs up neat in the garage so we can see what we got." When everything was out of the trunk, my father put his hands on his hips. "Your daddy ain't working this summer?" he asked Donny.

"He says he's got stuff around the house to do."

My father raised his eyebrows and nodded. "Jeb, get on some old clothes. We about to do battle."

"Why don't we start tomorrow?" I said.

"Cause we starting now."

I changed into old jeans and a tattered T-shirt, and

when I came back out, my father had two buckets, two jugs, and two scrub brushes laid out. He filled a quarter of each bucket with bleach, the fumes burning my eyes. "Bottom half of the house is yours, top half's mine," he said.

Faint gray streaks of mildew lay here and there on the white siding tiles, but my father scrubbed every inch as if rubbing out a fire. Donny got an old brush from our garage and helped until at 5:45 the Chevy cranked and revved across the street. Donny stood erect, dropped his brush and walked home as if in a trance. My father didn't seem to notice, nor did he notice that we worked through supper time since my mother was at work and not there to remind him. Around dark it started raining, cold and hard, but still he didn't slow down. When all our light was gone, we moved to the front where the porch light illuminated the house.

About nine-thirty my mother's ride brought her home from J.C. Penney's. She walked up under her umbrella. "What on earth are y'all doing?" she asked.

"Taking back our house," my father said from his ladder.

My mother looked at me like I might be able to explain, then asked if we'd eaten yet. "Harlan, do you know what time it is?" They didn't speak to each other again the rest of the night.

After supper I went straight to bed, my muscles waterlogged, and blew air from my nose, trying to expel the odor of chlorine. I wanted to stay awake until I heard Mr. Ramos's car, so I opened my window to the damp night and sat on the edge of the bed. The breeze brought a tinge of seared metal, bauxite, from the aluminum plant by the river. In the distance, flares from Esso and Ethyl blazed against the low sky. Water dripped from the eave of the house into puddles in our back-yard. I thought of a letter I'd gotten from Bob early on, a letter that joked about boredom and told how he'd thrown an army brownie against a truck 438 times before it broke. I imagined Bob helping us wash the house, my father criticizing Bob and Bob joking until Daddy stormed away. But then the images from the tape seeped into my mind—a man with no head, an arm on fire, Bob lowering a human leg into a sack. I stared at the white wall near the baseboard, trying to reconcile the images of my laughing brother with the voice I'd heard on tape. It was if the old Bob had died and spoken to me from a horrible other side.

After a while Mr. Ramos's car spoke through the night air. I lay on my stomach, staring at the baseboard and hoping the peaceful sound of the rain would bring the old Bob back into my head. Then I saw them on the white wall, several tiny spots like pox. I swung out of bed and touched the spots with my fingers. Mildew blooming in the dampness. I tried to smear them, but they wouldn't smudge. I pressed my palm against them. For a moment I thought I could feel them growing.

••

My father stayed home from work at the chemical

plant so we could finish cleaning the house. My mother reminded him that a new tropical depression was heading inland, but he didn't answer. All morning the clouds thickened, the humid heat surrounding us like a membrane. My father kept examining my work, sometimes pointing to a spot I had missed, although I never saw what he was pointing at. Donny came over and he and I moved away from my father to the opposite side of the house where I told him about Bob's tape. Then Donny told me that he'd gotten a letter from Tootie telling how the others in prison on possession charges had taken him in and helped protect him from the dangerous convicts. We wondered why Tootie and Bob had never been friends, wondered if things would have been different for them if they had.

At 11:45 when his father started the Chevy, Donny tried to act nonchalant, but his face blanched as if it and not my hands had been in the bucket. "I got to go with him to get new spark plugs," Donny said.

I watched Donny walk away, then went to my father's ladder.

"Why we cleaning the house before a storm?" I asked.

"When you have something you take care of it," he said.

"It ain't dirty."

"It's dirty, even if you can't see it. Now get on it."

He sloshed bleach onto the tiles and went on without looking at me. I remembered the time Bob, on his own, had cleaned the garage, putting away the scramble of tools on my father's work bench, straightening the scrap lumber heaped in the corners, scrubbing the oil stains on the floor. When my father came home from a double shift, he studied the garage, a scowl on his face. "You piled all my tools in them boxes?" he asked Bob. "I'll never find nothing now." He shook his head and walked off.

"You could've stopped him from going," I said to him up on his ladder. He knew immediately what I meant. His eyes widened with hurt in a way I had never seen before, then they darkened.

"He made his own mind up," he said.

That afternoon the storm drove us inside. My mother said she'd told him so but my father didn't look at her. Near 5:45 I opened the door to listen for Mr. Ramos's car. "Close that," my father said.

"In a minute," I said.

"I said now. I'm tired of you listening to that silliness." I slammed the door. "Boy, you want a whipping?" He went toward their bedroom where my mother was lying down. I heard the Chevy start. For some reason, it made me want to scream at my father. I walked down the hall and stopped outside the door.

"It ain't my fault, Winona," I heard him say.

"He wanted to make you happy," she said. "If you don't know that, you should." No sound came from the room for several seconds, then the door opened. My father walked past me as if I weren't there.

In my room, I smoothed my hand over my bed, the

spread damp beneath my fingers even though the house had been closed all day. Above the baseboard the spots of mildew were larger. I turned off the light and opened my curtain so I could see the pine needles just outside my window moving beneath the rain, could see reflections shimmering off the puddles in the backyard. It was out there that Bob had thrown me the football after rainstorms, taught me how to plant and cut on wet ground. Afterward we would slide and tear ruts in the grass, infuriating our father when he came home from work. I knew if Bob were home now, he'd be doing something about the rising water, even if only taking me out to walk in it.

I joined my mother at the picture window in the living room. Gray sheets of rain, illuminated by flashes of lightning, whipped the water standing in the road and edging into our yard. Flood warnings rolled across the TV screen. Weather radar showed even heavier rains moving through New Orleans on their way to us. My father came in and watched the screen, his hands on the back of my mother's chair, then went through the kitchen into the garage. I found him there, staring at the damp floor near the wall, his arms hanging at his sides. "Is it coming in?" I asked.

He jerked as though he hadn't heard me come out behind him. "Go back inside," he said, his voice sharp. From the kitchen, I heard him sliding scrap lumber into the rafters of the garage ceiling, heard the garage door being raised. "What's he doing out there?" my mother asked. She walked to the door, touched the knob, then shook her head and returned to the living room. Through the door window, I saw him sitting on an overturned bucket, watching the street.

At 11:45 I walked onto the porch to listen for Mr. Ramos's car and found my father standing calf-deep in the street near the drain. He scanned our yard and the yards nearest us where the water had moved halfway up to the houses. I waded out to him. "Ground just can't take no more," he said, rain pouring off the brim of his aluminum hard hat. Mr. Ramos's garage light was on, but I didn't see him.

"What we gonna do?" I asked.

My father shook his head. "Might as well get some sleep." His listless voice reminded me of Bob's on the tape. I wanted him to grab his shovel and go to the drain, to tell me to get a bucket and bleach, to do something. Instead, he turned to go inside. My mother stepped out onto the porch. He sat near her feet and pulled off his boots.

"You think it'll get in the house?" my mother asked him.

"Never has before," he said.

"We've never seen rain like this before."

With his right hand, he pulled against the fingers of his left. "One of y'all think you can stop it from raining, be my guest," he said, and went in the house.

I stayed where I was, my feet covered by water. Across the street Mr. Ramos hustled outside and bent over his bucket, watching it fill, I guessed, faster than he'd imagined it could. Their yard was lower than ours and the water had already reached their house. Donny's face peered through the back door window. "I'm going in," my mother said. I followed her, expecting her to argue or at least talk to my father, but both of them silently retired.

In the darkness of our living room, I sat in my father's chair and listened to the downpour, impossibly hard after so many hours. I pictured our house going under, all of us standing there, doing nothing.

••

Someone pounding on the door awakened me, but before I could move, my father opened it. "You gotta come," Donny Ramos said, his clothes laden with water, his hair wetted flat against his head. "Momma said to get you."

"Wait here," my father said, and surprised me by not asking Donny what was happening. I slipped on my shoes and my raincoat and joined Donny outside where a quarter inch of water covered our porch. The rain, though not as fierce as before, was still falling. "It's in our house," Donny said to me. "Daddy's in the garage."

When my father came out, we waded in, the water deepening to my waist as we descended to the street. Donny hurried ahead of us, the water, black as oil and smelling of gasoline and sewage, even deeper on him. Grass and leaves floated on the surface. "Be careful where you step," my father said, directing us away from the drain, but Donny plowed ahead.

As soon as we reached their driveway, I saw Mr. Ramos jacking the Chevy, the car leaning at a precarious angle toward the driver's side. The water covered the car's bumper even though the car itself was completely off the ground. Mrs. Ramos stood at the back door next to a dam of towels as high as her knees. "He won't leave that car," she said. "I'm raising what I can. I didn't know what to do but call."

"How much water you got in the house?" my father asked.

"A couple of inches, but it's still coming up."

My father pushed a fist against his mouth, then walked toward the garage. Mr. Ramos, drenched, glanced at us and continued jacking.

"You getting water in your house, Ramos," my father said.

"You came over to tell me that? I can see that."

Mr. Ramos stopped jacking, took a deep breath and ducked into the water. After several seconds his head came up next to the car. He inhaled and went under again.

"He keeps raising them standing jacks," Donny said.

Mr. Ramos popped up, leaned with his hands on his knees and took a deep breath. He flicked the directional switch on the jack, lowered it until the car rested on the submerged stand, then took the jack to the other side of the car.

"If you got some bricks, we can lift your furniture," my father said.

"There's a pile in the backyard," Mr. Ramos said. "Have at it." He locked the jack against the back bumper. My father took a step toward Mr. Ramos, then examined the Chevy. The space between the side wall of the garage and the car was much closer in the rear than in the front.

"Them jacks ain't high enough to get this car out of the water, Ramos. You can't even see if you're getting them firm under the supports."

"I don't have to see. I can feel."

Donny walked to the car and laid his hands on the hood while Mr. Ramos pumped the jack handle once more, the tilted car creaking. Donny lifted his hands and gaped at the car as if it were being magically levitated.

"Stay here," my father said to me. He started through the narrow space between the car and the wall.

"I didn't ask you to come over here," Mr. Ramos said. "I can take care of this myself."

"You got to come with me. We got to help your wife get the furniture up off the floor."

Mr. Ramos looked beyond my father as if he suddenly remembered his wife. "Go help your mother, Donny," he said.

"Stop acting crazy," my father said.

Mr. Ramos jerked as though stung, then stepped toward my father. "Crazy. Who you calling crazy?" He shook the jack handle. "You think I'm crazy?"

"Your house is going under. It's too dangerous messing around under this car." My father reached out and tried to grab Mr. Ramos's arm, but Ramos jerked away and pointed the jack handle like a sword.

"Who you think you are? You think you're better than I am?" He shook his head. "I've got something right here. I'm not letting it get ruined."

Mr. Ramos jabbed the bar into the jack and pumped double-time. The car wavered. He knelt, then went under again. My father made a move toward him, but the jack let out a shriek. The car lurched to the side, sending a wave against the wall. My father rushed the length of the car, his hand on the Chevy as if he could stop another shift, and reached underwater. Donny tried to get past me, but I grabbed him. He thrashed against me but I held on. In the narrow space, my father pulled Mr. Ramos from the water, my father's arms on Mr. Ramos's, and tried to move him out of the garage. They struggled a moment, a slow-motion dance, then Mr. Ramos threw off my father's grip. Mr. Ramos sloshed past the car and kept going on into the house. My father hesitated, then hurried through where Mr. Ramos had gone.

Donny stared at the house for a long moment, then he spun on the car, hit the hood with his fist and began pushing against it. I froze, believing for a second that the car was going to topple, believing that Donny could do that. My father hugged Donny from the rear, hugged him until Donny stopped resisting. "We got to help your momma," my father said, his voice quiet. "We got to go in and help her." Donny gazed toward the house, his expression disconnected and furious. Then he nodded and headed toward the bricks.

Once inside the Ramoses' house, I tried not to hear Mr. Ramos talking to himself in his room, Tootie's name a wail. Donny, Mrs. Ramos, my father, and I lifted the furniture onto bricks without speaking or even looking at one another. I wanted my father to speak, to at least break the silence and shame, and when he didn't I knew that he was scared, too.

After we finished, my father and I waded into the street again. Lights burned in all the houses now, people scrabbling to find whatever they could to elevate their belongings. My father walked ahead, not speaking, and even though I knew better, I said, "Mr. Ramos is nuts." He slapped me on the side of the head, not hard, but unexpectedly.

"Don't ever say that again," he said, and walked on.

I stopped in the street, the dark water to my waist. The low sky pulsed salmon from the plant flares burning even in the rain. My father's back moved away from me, the water sloshing before him. And at that moment I hated him, for hitting me, for making Bob go to war, for being an adult in a place that made no sense. But mostly I hated him for being weak in the way a child sees weakness, hated him for being unable to solve complexity with a simple gesture, hated him because when he'd held Mr. Ramos I had seen the limitations of strength.

"You coming?" he asked, holding open the screen door. I forced my legs to move through the water.

When we entered the house, my mother was mopping the quarter inch of water on the living room floor. It seemed impossible that it could be there. My father scratched his head and scanned the room, walked over and peered the length of the hall. "How long?" he asked.

"A half hour," my mother said. My father nodded, shoved his hands in his pockets and took in the scene as if he had to see every inch of the floor under water before he could comprehend any of it. He took his hands out and rubbed them together, then arched an eyebrow at my mother. "When it rains, huh?" he said. My mother and I glanced at each other. My father looked at me, his face breaking into a weird smile. He stomped his foot, making a small splash. "Y'all know. When it rains it pours. Can't argue that, can we?"

He slapped his hands together, the laughter taking him until he held his stomach. I moved away from him and looked at my mother. I had never heard him laugh like this, in an abandoned way that recalled Mr. Ramos wailing for Tootie. My father stepped toward me, grabbed me and pulled me to him. I pushed against him, but he held me, his body shaking against mine. He started to dance, water splashing onto the walls and furniture, my mother holding out her palms to tell him to stop. Then he pirouetted with me, lifted my feet off the ground, as the floor warped right there beneath us.

# Complicity

Mr. Park came out of our house wearing a brown suit, his Baton Rouge City Police detective's uniform, his body like a thick rectangle carved from an oak. He came close and leaned his large bald head toward me. "You best leave Ricky alone," he said. Ricky was Park's son, and he and I had fought almost from the day they moved in years before. Some days Ricky shot out of his house straight to me and told me to screw my father or much worse, things that shocked me because he was two years younger than I was. I had just turned twelve.

"Jeb," my mother said, standing on the porch. "Come inside."

"I'm talking to you," Park said. "You hear?"

"Yes, sir," I said.

Mr. Park sucked at his front teeth, glanced at my mother, then headed across the bright green lawn to his house next door. I tossed my basketball into the garage and followed my mother into our kitchen. "Sit down here, young man," she said, and took a seat across the table. Her pale blue eyes sparked like they had the time my brother, Bob, was arrested as a teenager for hitting black people's houses with eggs. "You are not to fight Ricky Park," she said.

"But, Momma—"

"I said no more."

"He picks fights with me."

"I don't care. You're his friend. He fights you because he's confused."

"If he starts it—" She reached over and pinched my face in her hand. She had only laid rough hands on me a few times in my life, and I didn't know why she was defending him. My cheeks were on fire.

"Every time you fight him, I'm going to whip you and then punish you. Understand?" She let go of my face, shifted in her chair, rested her hands on the table and intertwined her fingers. "I know it's not all your fault," she said. "Ricky is a mad boy. Sometimes when he's mad, he's not really mad at you. You have to hold back." Outside, a car door shut. My mother raised her eyebrows and leaned toward me again. "Do me a favor," she said. "Let's not tell your daddy or Bob that Mr. Park said anything to you, okay?"

"I ain't started any fights with him. He's acting like he used to."

"I know. You promise to do better, though?"

I went through the kitchen door to the garage where my brother, Bob, was carrying in a basket of dirty clothes. He had on one of his army shirts and his new black boots, the ones he wore with his police uniform. "Hey, stud," he said, talking out of the corner of his mouth opposite the cigarette he held. He hadn't smoked when he'd gone off to the army, but since he'd been back from Vietnam, it seemed he always had a cigarette. "Came to do some washing," he said. I brushed past him. When he came back out, I was bouncing chest passes off the wall. "Daddy wouldn't like you banging the garage like that."

"Daddy ain't home," I said.

"I see that." Bob reached out and slapped the ball down. "What's eating you?"

"Momma got on me for fighting Ricky."

"I didn't know you and Ricky still got in fights."

"He's been starting it again."

Bob ground his cigarette on the concrete. He scratched the side of his head, his fine, brown hair short the way it had been since he'd joined the police. "Jim know y'all been fighting?" he said, using Mr. Park's first name. "He must not," he answered himself. "He'd of been over here pissing Daddy off if he did."

"What am I supposed to do, Bob? Ricky messes with me, and Momma says I gotta take it."

Bob glanced past me at the Parks' house thirty feet away.

"Momma's right you shouldn't fight, especially not the way Jim and Daddy can go at it. I don't need that shit." Bob toed the concrete. "Tell you what. If Ricky gives you trouble, hit him right here." Bob pointed to my stomach. "Like this." In slow motion Bob uppercut me. He smiled. "Don't say I told you, but that'll cool his ass out."

••

Ricky pedalled his bicycle across their yard and into

ours. I had just cut the lawn, and Ricky sliced his front wheel into the soft pile of grass I was raking. He had gotten a fresh crew cut since I'd seen him a couple of days before, and his white scalp showed on the top of his head.

"Let's go ride bikes," Ricky said.

"I gotta finish this."

He let his bike fall at my feet, then grabbed hold of a mimosa branch and tugged at it.

"Get off that," I said. "My daddy doesn't want anything to happen to that tree."

"So?" Ricky said.

Only in the last few years had the mimosas begun to flower again. When I was four, a disease had plugged the arteries of all the mimosas in town, causing the trees to swell and split and bleed pungent yellow sap that attracted hornets. Ricky hoisted himself on a limb, cracking it. I pulled him away and checked the split. The limb would heal if left alone.

"Daddy's gonna be pissed if he sees this," I said.

"Piss on your daddy. Let's go bike riding."

"Why you got to be a twerp, Ricky?"

"What? I can't hear you. I'm deaf." He stuck his fingers in his ears and staggered into me.

"Cut it out," I said.

"What?" He cupped his hands behind his ears. "You suck donkey dicks?"

My ears burned, but I remembered what my mother had said. I turned my back. Behind me, the limb snapped. Ricky jerked and twisted at it. I shoved him away.

"You lick your daddy's ass," he said. "Lick, lick, lick."

"Get out of here."

"Lick, lick, lick, lick," he said, and lifted the end of his nose with his thumb. He launched a gob of spit on-to my cheek. My fists clenched, but I held off. With my shirttail, I wiped off the spit. He spat in my face again. "You chicken?" he said, his face twisting. "Buck, buck, buck."

I stepped forward and slugged him in the stomach. He stumbled backwards and dropped to one knee. "Shut up, Pricky," I said. He charged me and I hit him again, felt his stomach collapse as the wind left him. He crumpled and curled on the ground. "Pricky Fart," I said, standing over him. I had never felt so powerful.

"That's enough!" came Mr. Park's voice. He was strid-ing across the yard at us. "You done it now." He looked at Ricky. "Get up, boy," he said. Ricky struggled to his feet, still holding his belly. "Go hit him like he hit you." I balled my fists. Ricky hesitated. "Go! You ain't taking that from him."

I turned to go inside, but Mr. Park yanked the collar of my shirt and spun me around so close that I smelled coffee on his breath. "I say you could leave?" he said. "Hit him, Ricky." Ricky moved up to me. His eyes had hatred in them, but his face was different from a minute ago, not smartass this time. "Hit him!" Mr. Park said, and Ricky threw a punch that I deflected. Mr. Park held my arms. Ricky jabbed me in my tensed stomach. "Again!" he said, and Ricky hit me twice before Mr. Park released me. I fell to the ground for a few seconds, then I leaped at Ricky. Mr. Park lifted us both by our shirt collars. "Enough," he said.

My eyes met Ricky's, but his weren't really focused on me. Then I looked at Mr. Park. His mouth was smiling. "Kiss and make up," he said. He shook us. "Now." He pushed us together. Ricky licked my face and gave an odd laugh as I tried to hold my head away from him. Mr. Park pulled us apart.

"Jim!" came Mrs. Park's voice from their front porch. "Jim, you and Ricky come on."

"Get back in, Irene." Mr. Park gave Ricky a light slap on the side of the head. "Go with your momma," he said. Ricky picked up his bike, laughed and headed toward his house. Mr. Park released my shirt, but I knew I wasn't supposed to move yet.

"Jim," Mrs. Park said. Mr. Park stood between her and me, but I could tell her voice was closer. Mr. Park bent over so that his cloudy eyes glared near mine. "Next time you wanta hit my son, remember this," he said. Mr. Park stretched his neck to both sides and turned. As he walked past Mrs. Park, he said, "Inside." Mrs. Park looked at me like she was about to say something, then followed.

When they were gone, I beat the rake on the ground, flung it into the mimosa tree, then rode my bike to the school ground and climbed an oak. Once, before Bob had gone to Vietnam, he had argued with Mr. Park until my father came out. My father had pushed Bob toward the house, then quietly and intensely spoken to Mr. Park, Mr. Park smiling and nodding as the veins in my father's temple stood like vines. I wanted to tell Bob or my father what Park had done this day, but sitting in that tree I knew that I wouldn't.

••

My father set the nut on the damp garage floor and lifted the blade from the overturned lawnmower. Bob talked fast, glancing at me but talking toward my father. My father hadn't looked at Bob, though, and Bob's voice was louder than when he'd started. "So we got the nigger cuffed and his two brothers fought off and we're moving across the yard to the unit when the momma charges out wailing, this big woman, and starts clawing me down the arm." Bob took two quick slugs from his Coke. My father slid a pair of goggles over his head and slipped heavy gloves onto his hands. He flicked the switch to his wheel grinder and held the blade's metal edge to the spinning stone, letting loose a whine.

"My hands are full and my partner's telling the brothers to stay back, so I kicked the mother in the shin to keep her off," Bob almost yelled. "At that point I tossed the suspect in the car and shoved the woman again, while my partner cranked the unit. We tore out and, can you believe it, the woman chased us down the street." Bob wiped cottony spittle from the corners of his mouth, then tilted the Coke for a long drink. His left forearm was wrapped in medical tape. "My partner said we should've charged extra for family counseling." He laughed. I glanced toward the tail of sparks flying from the grinder. Bob nudged me. "Pretty wild, huh?" he said.

"You kicked her?" I asked.

"Citizens don't like their sons being cuffed."

My father turned off the grinder and held the blade's shiny edge near the light. The grinder's scream wound down like a tiny siren. "How's your arm?" my father asked.

Bob downed his Coke. "You didn't like my story, Daddy?"

"It ain't my kind of work."

"You'd rather I had one of them shit jobs I had right after I got back? Least now I get some respect."

My father set the blade on the counter, removed his goggles and gloves. "I ain't said nothing to make you mad, Bob."

"But you wish I'd do something else."

"You still got your GI bill."

"GI bill. I want to do something. That dude I picked up was wanted for armed robbery, Daddy. Armed robbery. Ya know, Jim Park made a special trip to tell me I did a good job."

Bob slammed his bottle on the counter and walked out. My father shook his head and knelt by the lawn-mower. He stabbed the blade with the rotor bolt and began to tighten the nut. I followed Bob to where he sat on the hood of his car, his feet twitching. The early summer sunshine made me blink. "You gonna eat lunch with us?" I asked. He shrugged. His body odor stung my nose, a sharp smell that made me think of the jungle. I couldn't remember the smell from before he went away.

"Do something for me," Bob said. He lit a cigarette. "Don't fight Ricky no more."

"Mr. Park told you?"

"He mentioned it."

"Ricky spit on me and I hit him like you showed me."

Smoke drifted from Bob's cigarette into my eyes. "Look, I know Ricky can be an asshole, can't we all, but this is important." I wanted to tell him about Mr. Park grabbing my shirt, about Mr. Park's face close to mine. "You mad?" Bob asked.

"It ain't fair. He can do what he wants to me, and I ain't supposed to do nothing."

"I know," he said. "It's just I owe Jim one. He helped me get on the force. It's the first good thing that happened since I got back." From the garage came the roar of the lawnmower. Bob thumped his cigarette against the wall.

••

I was sighted and ready to release the ball at the goal on the side of our house when I heard yelling, then rumbling and a crash on the wooden floor through the walls of the Parks' house. It was loud like something Ricky would do, but Ricky had been at his granmother's for days. I stopped. I thought I heard more rumbling, but I wasn't sure. A block away someone hammered metal on metal. A mockingbird and a blue jay screeched in our backyard.

About an hour later, Mr. Park came out dressed for work. He looked inside his suit jacket, opened the door to his car and paused. I kept dribbling and waved with my other hand. Depending on his mood, he usually either ignored me or said something he thought was funny like "Don't bruise that iron," but this time he fixed on me, his eyes steady. He jerked his head in acknowledgment, then ducked inside his car. He revved into the street and accelerated fast, much faster than my father ever did. I listened to his engine wind out until it blended with the other distant traffic, then I put up a long jump shot that clanged off the rim.

That night, blue lights flashed through the picture window of our living room. My mother and I, alone because my father was at work, rushed outside. Four police units were in front of the Parks' house and Mr. Park's car was in his drive. Just as we reached the Parks' yard, Bob's police car slid to a stop.

"Y'all hear?" Bob asked as he joined us walking. His hands rested on his pistol and his billy club. "Somebody broke in on Mrs. Park. Jim stopped home to eat and found her tied up."

We followed Bob to the Parks' sidewalk and halted in

the middle of several other policemen. The door of the house was open, exposing bright light inside. Neighbors hustled into the yard.

"What's the word?" Bob asked an older policeman with slicked-back red hair and a bulging stomach.

"She's roughed up, but she's okay. Looks like the nigger might've came in the back door." The policeman glanced at my mother and me. Bob introduced us.

"They need any help?" my mother asked him.

"No, ma'am. They're asking her some questions right now. They'll be taking her to the hospital in a little bit." The sergeant looked at Bob. "They might want to stand back."

My mother and I moved back out in the yard and stood with Mr. and Mrs. Badeaux and the Simmons girls. My mother's blond hair was tied back in a pony-tail. She had her front teeth over her lower lip, her hands locked together at the bottom of her throat. Police radios crackled as a crowd gathered to stare through the Parks' open door. I wanted to go stand with Bob, but he was near the porch with other police-men and neighbors who kept asking him questions.

In a few minutes Mr. Park escorted Mrs. Park out to the car, holding her by the elbow. She walked slowly, pressing an ice pack against her face. When she got to the passenger side of the car, she paused, lowered the ice and looked over the crowd. In the light from the cars and the house I saw her swollen left eye. Mr. Park put his hand to her shoulder, urging her into the car, but she stood several moments longer. She looked in our direction, making me want to shrink, but my mother lifted her hand to Mrs. Park.

After three police cars led the Parks away, Bob called us over to the porch where he stood with a short detective whose tie was striped purple and gold and had LSU in tiny letters on a football. "Your brother tells me you play a lot of basketball," the detective said to me. "You good as Pete Maravich?" He talked to me as if I was younger than I was. Bob winked. "This afternoon, you see any strangers in the neighborhood?" the detective asked. "Maybe a nigra man?"

"No, sir."

"You notice any cars going by slow, or bicycles with nigras riding on them?" The crowd in the yard had broken into clusters. Out in the street, Donny Ramos and a few other kids rode their bikes in tight circles.

"I didn't see anybody different," I said.

"Anybody go in or out this house, workman or something?"

"Mr. Park went to work, that's all."

The detective smiled. "Well, keep thinking about it," he said.

Bob and I went back over to our mother. She and Mrs. Park weren't close friends, but I could tell my mother was feeling for her. "What exactly happened, Bob?" she said.

"Far as we can tell, some nigger, probably one that Jim busted, broke in on Irene and tied her up with an electrical cord then beat on her."

"Is that all he did?" my mother asked. She glanced at me.

"We think he just hurt her. We figure all he wanted was to get back at Jim."

"Did Irene recognize him?"

"Evidently not. We'll catch the son of a bitch, though. Somebody must've seen him in the neighborhood. Until then, y'all keep locked up."

When Bob was gone and we were back at our house, I tried to remember if I had seen anyone. The noise from the Parks' house came to mind, but I didn't think it was important. Bob had told me someone had broken into the Parks' and that was enough. In our kitchen, I found my mother, her palms flat on the tile counter as she stared at the closed, pine cabinets. When she sensed I was behind her, she gave a start, then touched her hair. I had seen her scared that way only once, when we heard on the news that an explosion at Bob's base in Chu Lai had killed more than fifty men, not all of whom had yet been identified. I imagined a black man coming through the back door while my mother was alone. I walked over and hugged her.

••

My father slammed the front door behind him as my mother ran in place with Jack Lalane and I ground pecans. My father jingled the coins in his pockets as he paced back and forth. "Damn the man," he said. "I go over to ask if I can help and he barely cracks the door."

"Did you see Irene?" my mother asked, her breathing choppy.

"I could just see Park as little as he opened the door."

My mother ran faster, her footsteps rattling a plate and saucer on the coffee table. In time with Lalane, she began throwing stiff punches, one arm then the other.

"Is Ricky back yet?" I asked my father.

"I don't imagine they'll get Ricky for a few more days," he said. He glared at the TV. "I hate to say it, but I can see where somebody Park arrested might want to get back at him. You'd think they'd thought of a better way to do it, though."

"I called this morning," my mother said, her words jarred by her motions. "Jim said Irene didn't feel like talking. I'm making a pie for them."

My mother jumped up and down, higher than I'd ever seen her jump, shaking the floor. My father stepped to the table and set the cup upside down on the wooden surface. "I wonder what went on over there?" he said. He looked at me, his eyebrows frowning, then at my mother's back. She strained to jump higher, the wooden floor booming. "Winona," my father said, but she lifted herself with her arms, landed again with a bang. A picture on the mantle toppled. "Winona!" he said. My mother spun, knees bent, as if we'd snuck in behind her. "Stop it! You rocking the whole damn house." She wiped sweat from her cheek and stared as though she had no idea what he was talking about. My father exhaled through his nose, wheeled and strode down the hall. When I turned back to my mother, she was reaching for the ceiling.

••

That afternoon, Mr. Park set a lawn chair on their walkway and sat with a shotgun across his lap. I went to tell my mother about him, but as soon as I entered the kitchen she asked me to take the pie over. Mr. Park started watching me as soon as I came out of our house, but he watched as though he could see through me. About five feet from him, I held out the pie covered in plastic wrap. "Momma baked y'all this," I said. He stared for a while before he took the pie and set it on the ground.

"That's sweet of your momma."

"I'm sorry about what happened to Mrs. Park."

He shifted the pump shotgun on his lap. My father wasn't a hunter, so the only rifle I'd ever been around much was a .22 single-shot we used to shoot cans by the river. "Let's get you a chair," he said.

I didn't want to, but I followed Mr. Park into the dim garage. On the floor lay Ricky's banana-seat bike, its handlebars twisted so that the front wheel faced backwards like the head of an animal felled while running. The chairs were propped against the wall near the door to the backyard. "Grab one," Mr. Park said, and when I turned, chair in hand, Mr. Park was much closer to me, blocking my way. He nodded at the back door. "I figure the suspect come in there." His features were murky and his bulk loomed in the poor light. He knocked the long shotgun softly against his leg and ran his fingers beneath his nose. "Nobody fucks with my family and gets away with it," he said. I nodded, not sure what to say. He kept his eyes hard on me. Finally, he sniffed and walked out.

Back outside, a wasp hovered over the hedges lining the sidewalk, then disappeared into the tiny leaves. Once, I had reached into the bushes to retrieve my football and grabbed a whole nest. I remembered them boiling toward my fingers.

"Is Mrs. Park okay?" I asked.

"She will be." He sucked at something between his teeth. "How late you play basketball yesterday?"

"Not late. I didn't see nobody."

"That's too bad. I'd like to get my hands on him."

"You think you will?"

Mr. Park patted the stock of the shotgun, his ring clacking on the wood. "He comes back around here I'll blow his black ass away."

Behind us Mrs. Park stuck her head out the front door. Her eye was nearly swollen shut, her lip scabbed. I stood while Mr. Park stayed seated looking toward the road. "Hey, Jeb," she said. She touched her black eye. "I didn't know you was out here." I wanted to say I was sorry or make a joke so she'd feel better, but all that came to mind was an image of her tied with a cord. Mrs. Park came down the steps, her whole body stiff, but when I started to help she made me sit.

"You shouldn't be coming out here," Mr. Park said.

"I'm out here already," she said, and lit a cigarette. "It's nice out. Not too hot yet." Mrs. Park clutched her robe closed more tightly and stood looking at the side of Mr. Park's head. Mr. Park ran his tongue around the inside of his mouth, then scraped his cowboy boots on the sidewalk.

"You have to sit out here, Jim?" Mrs. Park asked.

"Yeah, I do," he said, looking at her for the first time.

Mrs. Park took a deep drag from her cigarette and exhaled.

"Momma made y'all a pie," I said. "Pecan."

"Tell her thank you. I'll call her tomorrow."

The menthol smell of Ben Gay drifted from Mrs. Park. Mr. Park cleared his throat.

••

"You ever get to sleep last night?" my father asked my mother. I had been awake when he came home from the plant after midnight, and the murmur of their talking had come through my bedroom walls until I drifted off.

"I dozed," she said.

My father folded and creased his lunch bag, getting ready to meet his ride. "Well, try and get some rest," he said. "We'll talk some more later." He kissed her on the cheek and went out.

My mother hadn't put on any makeup all morning and her complexion was paler than usual, her eyes unlined and small. After my father left, she went straight to their bedroom, and in a little while came out with her lips fiery red and a green-and-red floral scarf on her head. "I'm going to see Irene," she said. While she was gone, I threw a football at a tree in the backyard. Every hit damaged the leather some, but I kept throwing harder and harder and running faster and faster to get the ball until my chest strained and sweat dripped into my eyes. When my mother spoke, it startled me. She seemed about to cry. "Get in the car," she said, and I didn't ask why.

We went for a roundabout drive, my mother silent, and for one of the few times in my life I couldn't think of anything to say to her. After about an hour, she turned into Howell Park, a park my father had forbidden me from after the pool had been integrated several years before. I still rode my bike through the park, but my mother being there near black people made me nervous. We sat at a picnic table near the old jet fighter but a good distance from the pool where black kids thrashed in the water. A woman in a lime green suit sprang from the high board, arched her back and stabbed the surface with hardly a splash.

"I'd forgot how pretty it is here in the summer," my mother said. "Everything's blooming." Pink blossoms adorned the mimosas scattered at the edge of the playground and the sweetness of magnolias carried on the breeze. Several black teenagers at a table not far from us laughed loudly. I crumbled a dirt clod.

"You remember when that blew up?" she asked, nodding at the red brick building near the pool. One night not long after we had stopped going, someone dynamited the pool's dressing area.

"Uh huh. Daddy brought me and Bob to see the inside all wrecked."

My mother took the scarf from her head and shook out her hair. She scratched a fingernail on the wooden top of the table. "I think somebody told your daddy who used that dynamite."

"He told you that?" I asked.

"No. I just felt like he might've known."

"Then why didn't he tell?"

"Maybe he didn't think there was anything he could do. Nobody got hurt. Maybe he didn't think it was so wrong."

I wasn't sure why he should have told, except that not telling seemed somehow a lie. I poked the ground with a stick, then threw it.

"Why'd you tell me that, Momma?"

"I don't know. I want you to be careful."

"Of what?"

"I don't know that either. You have to answer that."

••

Bob held the hose while my father washed grease from

his hands. We had changed Bob's carburetor while Mr. Park sat fifty feet away, the shotgun in his lap, a brown Stetson shading his eyes. "Who the hell's he think he's keeping away?" my father asked as he dug a thumbnail at the dirt under his other nails. "He been out there three days now."

"You'd be out there if somebody beat Momma up," Bob said.

"Don't be so sure." Bob rolled his eyes at me as we followed my father into the kitchen. My father pulled the lever to break open the metal ice tray, then dropped cubes into three glasses, filled his with water, took a long drink and wiped his mouth with a shirtsleeve. "What'd them detectives find over there?" he asked Bob.

"What you mean?"

"Was things broke? Was anything stole? Did the man do something with the woman?"

"What're you getting at, Daddy?"

"I'm asking if you believe the story Park's telling."

My mother came and stood in the doorway, her arms crossed.

"Of course I believe it," Bob said. "What do you think happened? You got all the goddamn answers."

My father gave him the look that said don't talk that way in my house, but he didn't say it. "I want to know who Park thinks he's scaring with that shotgun. If some nigger beat Irene up, he ain't coming back this soon and

Jim knows it." I clenched my fists. Almost everyone I knew said nigger but that time it was like a sharp stick thrust at my eye. My father rattled the cubes in his glass. "Is that show for us in this neighborhood?"

"You in on this, Momma?" Bob asked.

"Me and your daddy just wonder what happened," she said.

"Right," Bob said. "You know he's hearing this," he said, and pointed a thumb at me.

"I know Park got you on the force," my father said, "but that don't mean you have to buy his story."

"Will you be quiet, Daddy, will you just shut up?"

"We're just saying what if it happens again," my mother said. "Maybe worse? What then?"

"It ain't gonna happen again," Bob said. "That bastard won't be back." Bob went to the sink, rinsed his hands and splashed water on his face. "I can't believe you think this too, Momma."

Bob marched out, leaving our parents staring at each other. When I moved, my father touched me.

"What we said stays in this house."

In the garage, Bob shoved the toolbox onto the shelf. He lit a cigarette and blew smoke straight up. "I love Daddy, but he sure is an asshole. He's even got Momma talking shit." Bob walked out to his car and waved at Mr. Park, then took his sunglasses from his pocket and put them on. He slid behind the wheel and cranked the engine.

"I heard something," I said to Bob.

"Huh?" Bob said, craning his neck to listen to his car.

"The day Mrs. Park got beat up. I heard yelling or something inside their house. Mr. Park was still there."

"Goddamnit." Bob hit both hands on the steering wheel. "What you heard was nothing."

"I heard something, Bob. It didn't sound right."

He grasped me by the arm. "Look, Jeb. Daddy's trying to fill your head with crap cause he don't like Jim. Don't you listen to what he says, all right?" My reflection stood strangely bright and tall on the green mirror of Bob's sunglasses. I couldn't see his eyes and his hand still held me. "All right," I said. I stepped back as Bob pulled out. In front of Mr. Park's house, he slowed and yelled. Mr. Park laughed and raised a hand. I went into the garage and looked through the kitchen-door window, saw my father shaking his head as my mother spoke. Around me, the air was musty and hot.

••

A reverse layup had just rolled off my fingertips when Ricky coasted in fast on his bike and skidded to a stop, leaving a black tire mark on the concrete. His cowlick curled over his forehead like a breaking wave and his lips were colorless from being pressed together. "You heard what that nigger did?" he said, then lifted his handlebars and bounced his tire on the concrete. I hadn't even known he was back.

"Yeah, I heard."

"Why didn't nobody see him?" He wrenched his hands on the grips. "If I'd been home, I'd of seen him."

He popped a wheelie and held it. He circled me, his front tire wobbling, then lost balance and cut sharply, the tire scuffing my calf. I grabbed the back of his seat and jerked him to a stop, my leg burning.

"That hurt, shitass," I said.

"You pussy," he said. "You was here. Why didn't you do nothing?"

Anger distorted his face, the same anger that had caused his father to make me feel small so many times. My arm tensed to knock him off his bike, then I realized the true weapon I had, the ugly accusation that didn't even have to be true. I pictured him more furious than ever before, pictured all the hatred he had ever known focusing on me in an instant. I let go of his bike.

He rolled it into the grass where it dropped, then knocked the ball from my hands. He retrieved the ball and charged like a fullback, his breathing snorts, but I sidestepped and shoved him. His knee hit the concrete with a hollow thud and he rolled over clutching his leg. "You fucker!" he yelled, tears bursting from his eyes. He leaped up and charged me again. I spun him and we both went down. Straddling his chest, I grabbed his wrists and held as he strained against my hold. The tears trailed through the down on the side of his face, a face bruised with redness from the pressure of his struggle.

"Stop it," I said, and stayed on him. After a couple of minutes he struggled less, although he kept cursing. It was possible he would try to hit me again, but I let him go anyway. He stood, his fists at his sides, and kicked the ball. He flung the tears from his cheeks, then dabbed a finger in the blood on his leg.

"I oughta kill you," he said.

"No you shouldn't," I said. I went over and righted his bike. "Let's get you a Band-Aid," I said, and to my surprise, he walked beside me to their garage.

In their kitchen, Mrs. Park washed Ricky's knee with a rag, then taped a Band-Aid across it. "What did you do?" she asked.

"I fell on my bike," Ricky said, and glanced at me.

"The walking wounded," she said. Ricky pulled his shorts up his stomach and limped around, bobbing his head and moving his tongue in and out until I laughed. Then we both sat at the kitchen table where Mrs. Park poured us some purple Kool-Aid and lit herself a cigarette. A black crescent curved under her eye. Below it her skin was yellow and blue. When she handed me my glass, I saw a thin bruise on her wrist.

"Is Mr. Park at work?" I asked.

"I finally sent him back," she said. She slid her chair from the table and went to the window. In the backyard, the wind rustled the fine leaves of the mimosa, the tiny blossoms fluttering like hair. "They look like little pink-and-white crowns," Mrs. Park said, and flicked an ash onto the windowsill.

"I climbed a big one at Mawmaw's," Ricky said. Mrs. Park nodded without looking at him.

I remembered when I was much younger, watching the hornets come to the dying mimosas. Thick sap had run from the trees, attracting the hornets with its sickly sweetness, and they had landed in swarms, their large yellow-and-black bodies like grotesque honeybees. I had only seen hornets a few times before, using their black stingers to kill cicadas in flight, but they came to the sick trees for days, moving across sap the color of pus until they were full, then taking to the air with a heavy drone.

"Daddy's gonna catch that nigger," Ricky said.

"Ricky," Mrs. Park said. "Shut up about that."

"Daddy's been sitting out front with his shotgun to let him know he better not come here anymore," he said to me.

"Jeb knows," Mrs. Park said. "He sat out there with him."

Ricky stared at his mother's back and thumped his glass a couple of times, then jerked his head and focused on the center of the table as if he had seen the moment when blows landed on her. I wondered what he knew and if he did know whether he could ever say the truth to himself. He showed his teeth. Around his upper lip was a small moustache of Kool-Aid.

"If that nigger comes back here, I'll kill him," he said.

Mrs. Park took a deep drag and exhaled. "Nobody's coming back," she said.

# Bonnie Ledet

I had dragged the cardboard refrigerator box of toys
from the garage onto the driveway and was dividing its
contents into three piles—keepers, junk, and Salvation
Army. Deep in the box I was finding things that went back
to when my older brother had lived at home, back to
when I was much younger than thirteen, what I was at
this time. I pulled out a cracked New Orleans Saints
helmet, a ragged Davy Crockett coonskin cap, and two
large tin cans with straps that we had used as Steve Canyon rocketpacks. My father had told me he was tired of
clutter around his work counter. He was irritable when
working the three-to-midnight shift, but I liked the shift
because it left my mother and me alone to go out for
milkshakes or play Chinese checkers or just talk. Lately,
though, we hadn't done many of those things because
she was still recovering from her first bout of lupus, which
had put her in the hospital then kept her bedridden for
a month.

I laid the tin cans on the junk pile, then saw three
kids, a boy and a girl about my age and a younger boy,
coming across the yard next door. News travelled fast in
our neighborhood, but I didn't know where these kids
had come from. The older boy led the way, smiling and

smoking a cigarette. He wore an army shirt with cut-off sleeves. Blackheads peppered his face.

"I'm Blane," he said, his Cajun accent so heavy it took me a second to understand his words. "This my little brother, Roland, and my sister, Bonnie."

"I'm Jeb," I said.

Roland was shorter and chunkier than Blane and stood with his hands plunged into his pockets and his shoulders slumped. As he stared at the toys on the concrete, his eyebrows slanted in a frown toward the bridge of his nose.

The girl, Bonnie, hung back, wiry inside a faded paisley summer dress. Her short black bangs were pulled to the side and held by a plastic barrette. Her nose was pointy, her cheeks sunken below high ledges of bone. Now that she was nearer, I saw that she was probably the oldest of us.

"Our old man and us, we just moved in," Blane said, then ground his cigarette on the drive.

"My daddy won't like it if you smoke," I said.

"That's cool," he said, and pointed at my basketball lying on the grass. "You mind if I shoot?" he asked. "Roland, he ain't good as me."

"Kiss my ass, Blane," Roland said, scowling out of proportion to the remark. He bent back the fingers of one hand against the palm of his other. "Where you got all that stuff?" he asked me.

"I had most of it a long time. I'm throwing all that out."

"I can have this?" he asked, picking up the football helmet.

"Leave that alone," Blane said. "Them ain't no baby toys."

Roland took a swing at Blane's arm and missed. Roland squeezed the helmet down over his head, and he and Blane started shooting, their movements awkward and foot heavy. Bonnie stood about fifteen feet away, hugging her waist as she inspected my house and yard, her head slightly tilted toward the ground as though she was afraid of getting caught.

"Where y'all from?" I asked her.

She looked sideways at me, her eyebrows arched. "Dulac."

"Where's that?" I said.

She rubbed her forearm and bit her lip.

I asked, "Is it close to New Orleans?"

"It's down by Houma. Close to the gulf."

"I've never been to Houma."

Blane yelled, laughing, and bounced the ball hard off Roland's head. Roland ran after him, but Blane grabbed Roland's face mask and kept him at arm's length.

"Fucker," Roland said. I thought they were about to fight. Bonnie sat and crossed her legs in the thick, early fall grass. Her skirt slid midway up her thighs, pale and muscled. She plucked blades of grass and tossed them to her side in small, violent movements until there was a fist-sized divot in front of her.

"When did y'all move in?" I asked and sat across from her.

"Yesterday," she said.

"Y'all have a big moving van?"

"Why you need to know?"

I shrugged. "Just asking."

I heard the front door open behind me, my mother coming out to sweep the porch. Bonnie stood, smoothed her skirt over her thighs and touched her fingers to her barrette.

"Blane, Roland, time to go," she said.

"You go on," Blane said.

"Daddy ain't gonna like it we not there when he gets back."

"Fuck Daddy."

The sweeping stopped. I stood, too.

"Blane," Bonnie said. "Don't get me in trouble."

Blane spat into the grass.

"Come by and get us for school," he said to me. "We live around the corner." Bonnie was already walking away, her hands clenched at her sides. With each step she took, the curve of her hips showed through her dress. At the corner Blane saluted, then punched Roland in the shoulder, but Bonnie didn't look back.

"Who were they?" my mother asked, close to me, her arms crossed. Her hair rose in a bouffant, a style she'd started after her illness. She thought it made her face less gaunt, but I thought it brought out the faint circles under her eyes.

"They just moved in one of the rent houses," I said. "They're coonasses."

"Don't say that word," she said.

"Mr. Badeaux says it." He was our Cajun neighbor.

"It hurts people's feelings. You don't say it."

She knelt next to the pile of junk and lifted the edge of a toy car garage whose rusty decks were concave from where I'd sat on it when I was two. She ran her fingers over the surface, blue veins standing on the back of her hand.

"I remember the look you had on your face," she said, smiling. "You thought crushing this was the cutest thing. I wish your daddy didn't want to throw these out."

"I'm just throwing out the broken ones. I'm keeping all the good stuff."

She stood and scratched the place on her hand where small blood clots still lay beneath the skin. The doctors had thought the rash was an allergic reaction to insect repellent my mother and I had used at a drive-in movie late that summer, and it would be years before we realized it was the first sign of her lupus. She moved her hand against the grain of my hair, then down to my neck. She squeezed, the ends of her long nails slightly digging in. It was an odd way for her to touch me, and I recoiled a little. She took her hand away.

"I want you to keep that," she said, and pointed at the crumpled garage. "I know it's trash, but it makes me think of when you were younger."

••

The next morning I walked to school between Bonnie and Blane. Bonnie wore a brown dress that fit too tightly everywhere except underneath her arm, where I could see her white brassiere. Blane smoked a cigarette and asked if there were any girls in the neighborhood, if I had a friend with a car, if I'd ever been drunk.

"My brother gave me some wine once," I said.

"I been drunk about a hundred fucking times," Blane said. "I get drunk all the time."

"You lying, Blane," Bonnie said.

"No, I ain't. I love to get fucked up."

"Quit saying that word," she said.

"What word? Fuck? It bother you, Jeb?"

"Don't say it in front of my parents."

"It hurts their ears, huh?" Blane kicked a rock. "All right, Bonnie, listen up. No smoking, no drinking, and no cussing at Jeb's house. You got that?" Blane leaned over and gave me a mock whisper. "Bonnie think she our momma."

"Shut up, Blane. You ain't funny." Bonnie hugged her notebook. The morning sun exposed a light sideburn of down on her face.

"Check it out," Blane said, pointing. Up ahead was the Stop N Go parking lot where long-haired boys with homemade ink tattoos and heavily made-up girls in hip-hugger jeans smoked cigarettes before school. "See y'all," Blane said, and headed off.

"Blane," Bonnie said. "Daddy wants you to go to school."

"Y'all tell me about it later." He winked at me.

Bonnie's jaw muscle flexed. "You know them people?" she asked me.

"Some of them. They go to school sometimes."

"Blane always looking for trouble. Something loose in his head."

I laughed, and after a second Bonnie smiled.

"I wish Blane didn't say that in front of your momma yesterday," Bonnie said. "She's pretty."

"She was real sick a month ago. She had to quit her job at Penney's." I remembered her in the hospital, her face so puffy her eyes were slits, her skin so sore I could only touch her hair.

"She's well now?"

"She's better. She still gets tired and her skin hurts her."

I was about to ask about Bonnie's mother, but a girl screamed and ran past us, a boy making monster grunts chasing her until the crossing guard halted them at the corner. Bonnie covered her mouth and laughed. It was the first time she'd seemed my age.

••

In Louisiana history Bonnie sat in the row next to me one seat ahead. While the teacher lectured about explorers, I noticed how in profile Bonnie's chin and nose curved ever so slightly toward each other as if trying to touch in front of her lips. I traced the swell of her calf, studied the movement of her shoulder blades beneath the material of her dress, followed the lay of the fine, dark hair on her forearms. Her body was older than most of the other eighth-grade girls, and when she leaned and reached inside her desk, I saw the cone of her bra pointing away.

After school we walked to her house, where she stopped at the end of the driveway. I was hoping she would ask me in, but she stood until I asked if we could sit on the porch. Her eyebrows dipped together, and she did a slow take on her house as though she expected to see someone she hadn't seen before. Then, without speaking, she walked to the cement steps, sat and pulled her knees close to her chest.

"Your momma didn't move down with y'all, did she?" I asked.

"She died when I was nine," Bonnie said, then watched to see my reaction. "I had to stay home, take care of Roland cause Daddy was gone so much."

"Is that why you're in eighth grade?"

"Yeah, that's why. Something wrong with that?"

"I just thought you were older than me, that's all."

She blinked her eyes and drummed her fingers on her knees.

"I'm sorry," she said. "I thought you meant something."

"Why was your daddy gone?"

Bonnie focused on the ground, moving her eyebrows up and down as if working the words into her mind. "He had a boat," she said slowly, not looking at me. "One of them big fishing boats people pay to go on."

"Cool," I said. "Does he still have it?"

"It got tore up in a storm. That's why we had to move down here." She rocked back and forth, then stood. "I got to get dinner."

"You mind if I ask you something?" I said. She shook her head. "What happened to your momma?" Her gray eyes pierced me. "I'm just wondering."

"She drowned. She was out on the boat and something happened. She got knocked over the side."

"Really?"

"You don't believe me?"

"I believe you. It sounds terrible."

Bonnie unlocked the door.

"Was your daddy there?" I asked.

"He didn't see it. They didn't find her." She turned the doorknob.

"You mind if I ask you something else?"

"Depends on what it is."

"You ever get mad at her?"

"At my mother?" She searched the porch as if she'd dropped the answer. "I used to. Once in a while, I guess. It was a long time ago." She disappeared inside.

I looked at the gray concrete of the steps and thought of my mother dead, covered with a sheet in her bedroom. My mouth went dry.

At home I found Dulac in the atlas, a tiny circle near the end of a thin map road far south of Baton Rouge. The ragged coast wasn't far away and the land near Dulac was sprinkled with exotic-sounding bodies of water— Lost Lake, Four League Bay, Bay Junop—and French towns—Chauvin, Bourd, Cocodrie—whose names I wasn't always sure how to pronounce.

"What're you looking at?" my mother asked, laying a hand on my shoulder. Her nails were dark red.

I pointed at the map. "That's where Bonnie's from."

"That girl from yesterday?"

"Yes, ma'am. I walked to school with her. I like her."

"Have you been down at her house?"

I nodded. My mother took her hand from my shoulder and stepped around to my side. She had on a brightly flowered blouse I hadn't seen in a long time. She clicked her nails on the tabletop.

"Were her parents there?"

"Her daddy wasn't. Her momma's not alive anymore."

My mother's blue eyes widened for a moment. "How old is this girl?"

"I think she's almost fifteen. She's in my grade, though."

My mother touched her throat. "Well, I don't want you in that house when her daddy's not home."

"We were just on the porch."

"I said in the house." She put a hand to her temple and shut her eyes.

"You okay, Momma?"

She patted my shoulder. "I'm just tired. I went through my closet and got rid of some of my drab clothes." She posed a moment like a model, showing off her blouse, then touched her forehead. "I think I'll lay down a little while. Maybe later we can go get a hamburger or something."

After she left the room, I stared at the atlas again. I imagined Mr. Ledet's boat, a sleek yacht with Bonnie standing near the bow, her hair blown back, a school of dolphins leaping from the water. After a while I tiptoed down the hall to my mother's room and peeked in. She lay flat on her back, her arms at her side, her mouth open, snoring. I wanted to turn her on her side to stop the noise. Instead I sat on the wooden floor and thought of being on that boat with Bonnie, its sharp prow cutting the green waves as we headed away from shore.

••

As I waited for Bonnie in front of the school, I schemed to get her to invite me inside her house. Over two weeks had passed since we met, and even though we had been walking to and from school every day, I still hadn't been farther than her porch. I was thinking maybe I could start coughing and tell her I needed some water when a familiar car horn sounded. Parked in the circular drive behind the last school bus was our Galaxie 500, my mother waving to me as kids strolled past. I glanced to see if Bonnie had come out of the building yet, then walked over.

"What are you doing, Momma?" I asked through the passenger window. Thick makeup gave her face an unnatural beige color. Heavy streaks of rouge angled like war paint across her cheeks.

"I was out shopping and I thought I'd take you and your friend to the bakery." She hadn't taken a friend and me to the bakery since fourth grade. Bonnie came out, and I waved to her.

"I don't know. I kind of wanted to walk."

"It'll be fun, Jeb. Plus I'll get to meet this Bonnie you've been talking about."

Bonnie stopped several feet from the car. I told her what was happening.

"I better not," she said. "My daddy's supposed to be home early."

"It won't take long," my mother said. "I can explain it to him. Here, y'all get in the front."

Bonnie exhaled through her nose, then slid onto the seat between my mother and me. In the car my arm and leg tingled against Bonnie's, but she stared straight ahead. The odor of my mother's hair spray filled the car, and I kept my nose to the window, wondering if Bonnie would think my mother taking us to the bakery was queer. When we passed the Stop N Go, we saw Blane kissing a girl in a purple tube top. Bonnie looked at her lap and scraped her chewed thumbnail across the grain of a textbook.

"Has Jeb told you anything about me?" my mother asked, smiling.

Bonnie glanced at me. "He said you been sick."

"He did?" my mother said, her smile leaving. "Well, I'm as good as new now. I'm going to get another job soon." My mother tilted the rearview mirror toward her and moved her head back and forth. She turned on the radio and hummed along until we reached Delmont Pastries, a small place across the street from my old elementary school. She ushered us in, then stood slowly scratching the back of her hand as she examined the cakes and pastries on display behind the glass counter.

"Jeb, Bonnie, come see," she said.

I touched Bonnie's hand, and we walked over. My mother pointed at a cake with buccaneers and a wooden ship on top.

"Remember your pirate birthday?" my mother asked. "We put your presents in a treasure chest and had chocolate that looked like gold coins."

"Let's get something, Momma. Bonnie needs to go home." My mother frowned and ran her teeth over her bottom lip, leaving lipstick on her front teeth. She ordered three chocolate éclairs, and we sat at a small table. My mother dipped a finger into her icing, placed it in her mouth, then picked up her éclair and took a full bite. I pushed my thumb through the top of my éclair and felt the cold filling inside. When I cleaned my thumb on a napkin, I saw my mother looking at me.

"Jeb told me your daddy came here to find work," my mother said to Bonnie. "What did he do down there?"

I had already told my mother what Bonnie had said, and I hoped she was making small talk, but her tone made me shift in my seat.

"He worked some different jobs. He worked on drilling rigs sometimes."

I set my éclair on the table.

"And your momma passed away?"

Bonnie cut her eyes at me. "She died in a car wreck. Her and my daddy was out one night."

"I know that's hard," my mother said. "My momma died when I was a little girl. My older sister raised me. You must be very strong." My mother laid a hand on my wrist. "Did Jeb tell you he took care of me when I was sick?"

"Momma," I said.

"Sorry," she said. "But it's good we're close. A lot of families aren't."

Bonnie pressed a napkin to her lips. "I got to get home," she said and pushed her chair back.

"Let me take you," my mother said, but Bonnie was already going toward the door. "Go catch her," she said to me.

"Why'd you ask those questions?" I said. "I already told you about all that."

My mother wiped her mouth, leaving a red stain on the napkin.

"I didn't believe what she told you."

"You wanted to catch her in a lie."

"I wanted to hear it myself."

I wheeled and went out after Bonnie. As I crossed Winbourne Avenue I heard my mother call my name, but I didn't look back. Bonnie was striding across the schoolground. When I fell in beside her, she didn't look at me. I wanted to apologize for my mother, but seeing Bonnie's frown made my anger shift to her.

"Why'd you lie?" I said.

"I got to get home," she said. "My daddy don't like me being late."

"Tell me why you lied."

She stopped and faced me. "I like what I told you better. It ain't no big deal."

We walked again, not as fast. My mother slowed as she passed in the car, but when I wouldn't look at her, she drove away.

"Your momma don't like you with me," Bonnie said. "Why'd you tell her what I told you?"

I almost told the truth, that I eventually told my mother most things that happened to me, but I didn't say anything. Neither of us spoke again until we stopped in the street at her house.

"Why don't you ever ask me in?" I said. Her father's green Malibu sat in the driveway. Her jaw muscles worked in and out.

"Daddy don't like nobody in the house," she said. "Maybe when he's gone."

"I just want a glass of water," I said.

The screen door opened and Mr. Ledet stepped onto the porch. Khaki pants were all he had on. He was short and stocky, his muscular chest black with hair, his nose pointy like Bonnie's. In his hand was a cup of coffee. Half of his index finger was gone. "Bonnie," he said, but it sounded like "Bon A."

"I got to go," Bonnie said. At the door she had to duck under her father's arm. His eyes went right into her. He sipped from his cup, his face expressionless as he looked at me. "You go home," he said, then went back in.

I walked fast, away from the Ledets' house and ours, toward Hurricane Creek, a deep drainage ditch that snaked through our neighborhood. I shimmied down the steep side and sat on the slanted concrete near the bottom where a stench hovered above the stagnant water. The mouth of the pipe was snarled with trash—tree limbs, a broken chair, a deflated football—washed there by the rush of storm water. I hurled a chunk of concrete into the water.

A week after my mother had come home from the hospital, her fever returned, rising even after I'd put cold cloths on her and given her aspirin. I wanted to call my father at work, but my mother said he'd missed too much work already. I held her head as she vomited into the crescent-shaped pan, the acid odor burning my nose. Her flushed face went pale, even the raspberry welts, and I kept talking to her, stroking her hair, hoping she would open her eyes again. When she finally looked at me she said, "Goddamn this. Goddamnit I thought I was okay," words like none I'd ever heard from her, words that made me certain she was going to die.

••

I was dribbling my basketball a few days later when Blane came up the driveway, smiling, a cigarette dangling from the side of his mouth.

"You know where Roland at?" he said. "His school called Daddy at work, said Roland beat up some kid. Daddy mad as hell." Blane flicked ashes, then cupped the cigarette to hide it.

"I ain't seen him," I said. "You know why they fought?"

"Boy must've fucked with Roland. Roland don't start things, he finish 'em, though."

"There he is," I said, and pointed at Roland, who was coming from a clump of tall bushes across the street two houses down. His thumbs were hooked in his pockets, his jaw shoved forward.

"Shit, he was hiding," Blane said. "Roland, you was in them bushes?"

"I was thinking," Roland said.

"What that boy did to you?"

"Told me I couldn't read."

"You hit him?" Blane asked.

Roland touched his nose. "One time, right there."

Blane and I laughed, but Roland frowned at us.

"Daddy gonna whip your ass," Blane said.

"Shit on Daddy," Roland said. "Give me a cigarette."

"Jeb don't want us smoking here."

"You smoking," Roland said.

"How long you suspended for?" I asked.

"A whole fucking week. Principal say she going to teach me to act good. I told her I still ain't taking no shit."

"Boy, Daddy gonna hit you. Bonnie ain't gonna be able to stop this."

Roland stared straight ahead, tears welling up, then walked off toward their house. Blane wiped a fake tear for my sake, then went after Roland. Blane nudged him, tried to put an arm around Roland's shoulder, but Roland blocked it.

"Jeb, come here a minute," my mother said from the backyard corner of the house. Her left hand was covered with black soil, her right hand held a small rake with three claws. She'd been turning dirt in her small garden and had overheard everything we'd said. I banked in a shot, then slapped the ball into the grass before I walked to her. It was a warm day and her face was splotched pink as though she had fever again. Her blouse stuck in wet patches to her chest and the tops of her breasts.

"I don't want you near that house anymore," she said. "It's not good for you."

"You don't like Bonnie, that's it."

"She doesn't have a mother. Most of her life she's been by herself with those boys and a man who hits them. That girl knows a lot more than you do."

"That's why I like her."

She pointed the hoe at me. "I'm telling you not to go down there. End of talk." She walked back to the garden, lowered onto her knees and stabbed the dirt.

"You can't stop me," I said.

She looked up. Her chest rose and fell with the deep breaths she was taking. For a moment I was afraid she was working too hard, but I didn't feel like taking care of her then.

"I'm your mother," she said.

"Then why don't you act like it."

She narrowed her eyes at me. I took a step forward, wanting to take back what I'd said, but I didn't take it back.

••

The next morning I waited in front of Bonnie's house past the time she was supposed to show. The Malibu was in the driveway, but I knocked anyway. After the third knock, I heard heavy footsteps and moved back a little, bracing for Mr. Ledet, but the venetian blinds on the front window rattled, a dark slit opened and closed, then the footsteps receded. I made a fist to hit the door once more, then jumped off the porch and stormed toward school.

That afternoon, Bonnie was on her porch, wearing shorts and a low-cut shirt that showed freckles on her chest. Tied on her head was a red bandanna that hid her hair and caused her eyes to stand out from her face when she pulled on her cigarette, something I'd never seen her do. On her thigh I saw three bruises, each the size of a fingertip.

"Daddy said don't bang on the door." She pressed the arches of her bare feet together.

"Why didn't you answer? I wanted you to go to school."

"I ain't going to school no more. It's stupid. What you

learned there?" Bonnie struck a match, raised it near her eyes and blew it out. "Your momma's jealous."

"No, she ain't. She's my mother."

"So?" Bonnie took a last drag, then thumped the cigarette into the yard.

"Is your daddy here?"

"Work called him at noon." She struck another match and touched it to the rest of the foldover book so near the bridge of her nose that her eyes flamed when the matches ignited.

"Where's Roland?" I asked.

"Daddy ran him off hitting him." She examined my face. "You want to come in?"

"Inside your house?"

She laughed and stood.

Their house was hot and stale, without the exotic smells I'd expected, of roux and etouffee and fried garfish, like those at our neighbors', the Badeauxs. In the living room was a portable TV and a worn vinyl recliner with strips of silver duct tape on the seat. The walls were blank except for a framed photo of the family when Mrs. Ledet was still alive. Bonnie's mother looked like Bonnie except with a more rounded face. She looked younger than my mother, and I touched the glass without thinking. When I turned, Bonnie's lips were tight.

"You want some water?" she asked, and walked off. While Bonnie was in the kitchen, I wandered down the short hall. Through an open door I saw her father's room, his queen-sized bed covered by a tangle of sheets. Bonnie brushed past me, shut the door, and handed me my water.

"This is my room," she said, leading me across the hall. The only furniture was a wooden chair, a single bed without sheets, and a small chest of drawers. Atop the chest sat a round handheld mirror, a pair of scissors, and a bottle of rubbing alcohol. On the floor lay clumps of hair.

"You cut your hair?" I asked.

"No, it just fell out." Bonnie unscrewed the lid of the rubbing alcohol, sniffed it and recoiled. "You want a sip?" she asked, then shoved it under my nose. I pushed it away. She closed the bottle and dropped it back in the drawer.

"Let me see your hair," I said.

"Why should I?"

"I want to see what it looks like."

She took a transistor radio from one of the drawers, turned it on and moved across the room. "Your daddy ever hit you?"

"He used to whip me with a skinny belt," I said.

"Where he hit you? On the ass?"

I nodded. "Did your daddy hit you?"

Bonnie snapped her fingers to the music.

"You like to dance?" she asked.

"Dance?"

"Come on." She grabbed my wrist and pulled me across the hall into her father's room, my glass sloshing water. A basket of dirty work clothes reeked of sweat and chemicals. Next to the basket lay a white nightgown and some girl's underwear. When I looked at Bonnie, she had the radio pressed to her chin, her fingers white from gripping it so hard. She snatched the glass from my hand, plopped it down and made me step with her onto the bed. She turned up the music, kicked the covers and pillows to the floor, squeezed my wrists and bounced. I grasped her hands, and we flew, our heads almost touching the low ceiling, the bed creaking as Bonnie's wild laughter spilled over me. As we jumped I spun us and we turned a slow circle, gripping each other more tightly.

Suddenly she stopped, put a hand to my mouth and turned off the radio. Down the hall came footsteps. Blane stuck his head around the corner, then stepped in.

"What you doing?" he asked Bonnie. "You know it ain't cool Daddy catch him in here."

"The hell with Daddy," Bonnie said.

Blane flung his hair away from his glassy eyes. "Where Roland went?" he asked.

"He left this morning," Bonnie said.

"Damn. Where Daddy at?"

"He went to work. Leave us be."

Blane smiled at me. "Don't let my old man catch you," he said, and knocked twice on the wall. We heard him slam the front door.

"I know Blane stoned," Bonnie said. "I hope Roland don't start that." I stepped off the bed, but Bonnie stayed.

She touched the depression at the base of her throat. "You like me," she said.

"Yeah," I said. "I like you a lot."

She put her hand on my shoulder and hopped down. Her hand still on me, she reached with the other and removed her bandanna. Her hair was mutilated, the same length as before in some places, her scalp visible in other places, as if someone had ripped out hanks of it.

"Your daddy did that?" I said.

"I did it. You like it?"

"No I don't like it. Why'd you do that?"

She looked at the bed, then jerked her head as though she'd been slapped. She took my hand and ran it over her head, the bristles sharp, the longer hair soft and fine. The bandanna was still knotted, and she slid it onto my head, her thumbs pressed to my temples.

"You ever kiss a girl?" she asked.

"Not really."

"You want to kiss me?"

I nodded. She placed her mouth on mine. When her lips opened, I opened mine, too, let her tongue, thick and dry, come inside, the taste of cigarettes bitter and sharp. The second time I tried to use my tongue, but she took a step back, glanced over my face as if looking for some minute thing, then gently pushed me so that I sat on the bed. She sat sideways on my lap. I put my arms around her and hugged her, the small circles of her breasts against me, the warm skin of her cheek on my cheek.

"You can touch me," she said, and I slid my hands

under her shirt, over the tense muscles of her back and the knobby ridge of her spine. Her breathing was loud and close to my ear, and I felt wild and bigger than I was, moved my hands up to her shoulder blades, then around to her breasts, firm and soft at the same time like nothing I'd ever felt. She made a slight noise like pain and gripped me tighter, but her cheek moved from mine and she stood.

"You got to go," she said, and a small bolt of lightning went through my head.

"Is somebody here?" I asked. There was a swirl around her. She took the bandanna from my head, put it back on hers and went to her room. I followed her, but she kept her back to me.

"You didn't like it?" I asked, confused, thinking there was something I should do, but only wanting to touch her again. I took a step toward her, and she turned and pointed two fingers.

"Go on," she said.

"Your daddy made those bruises on your leg, didn't he? He hit you like he hit Roland. I want you to come to my house."

Bonnie smiled, hugging herself, but it was a smile close to crying. She put her hands on her head. "I did this. I took my scissors and did it. That fucker's gonna see. Now get on out."

As I went down the hall I heard her start crying. The feel of her skin and hair was still on my hands, the taste of her mouth still in my mouth. I walked out of her house, down her street toward mine, the world around me shut away as though I was in a tunnel. Inside our garage I stopped. A beam of sunlight slashed through the dirty window and across the dank room. Through the wall came the muffled babble of the TV like a voice beneath a blanket. I imagined Mr. Ledet's hand swinging hard against Bonnie's face. He pushed her to the floor, his hand gripping her thigh, his heavy body on top of hers.

I threw a punch into the wooden wall, then another and another, then I was kicking a metal gas can and plastic jugs of toluene, punching the wall again. "Stop it!" I heard my mother's voice yell and her hands pulled my arms, but I flung them off and kicked the washer, the hollow metal booming until she grabbed my shirt.

"Leave me alone!" I said, jumping back. "Don't touch me!"

"You stop it!" she said and held out her flattened hand. "You've been at her house!" She balled her fists.

I backed away. "What's wrong with you?" I said. "You're scaring me."

She stopped. The beam of light bleached her skin. She opened her fists and raised her hands, looked at the backs of them with disgust. She walked over to the steps by the kitchen door and sat. Her whole body looked tired, as if she'd been running ever since the rash had bloomed on her.

My hands were bruised and bleeding, my arms quivering. I walked over and sat next to her. After a minute she took my hands with her fingertips.

"We need to put something on that," she said, but we didn't move.

••

The next morning I knocked at Bonnie's even though the car was in the drive, then did the same again that afternoon. Later that night, after my father came home and went to bed, I snuck out to Bonnie's house, the night humid and cool. Mr. Ledet's car was still there, the porch light was off, but all the inside lights burned yellow through the blinds. On the side of the house, I listened beneath the high windows, but all I heard was the distant sound of traffic.

The next morning I knocked again, but when no one answered, I banged, twenty or thirty times. Blane jerked open the door. He was in his underwear. One eye was cut and swollen. "Shit! What you want?" he asked, a hand laid flat on his ribs.

"Jesus. Your old man did that?"

"You always asking questions." He rubbed a hand over his face. "I tried to stop him hitting Roland, so he switched off."

"You hit him back?"

"I tried. He's a tough fucker, yeah."

When I didn't say anything, he motioned me inside and led me to the kitchen. The linoleum floor was cracked and curling. Blane turned on the burner beneath a kettle. He pressed a filter into the drip pot and poured ground coffee into it.

"You drink coffee?" he asked. I shook my head. "Bet

my old man wish he didn't." He took an apple from the fridge, cut it with a thin-bladed filet knife and gave me half. We sat.

"Where's Bonnie?" I asked.

"At the hospital."

"She's hurt?"

"She's with Daddy." He smiled. "You fucked her?"

"Shut up, Blane."

He laughed, then grunted like an old man when he rose to pour the water.

"Did you hurt him when you hit him?" I asked.

"No, man. Bonnie put rubbing alcohol in his coffee. Fucked him up."

"Is he gonna die?"

"Nah. He's too mean to die."

Blane took a cup from the sink and turned on the hot water. He scrubbed the rim with his finger.

"He knows Bonnie did it?" I asked.

"She told him. His stomach cramped real bad, and when the ambulance pulled up, she said she wasn't gonna take him messing with us no more." Blane poured the water into the pot. The coffee dripping sounded like the ticking of a tiny clock. We each ate our apple half until Blane looked at me with the most serious expression I'd ever seen on his face. "You know about Bonnie and my old man," he said.

I tossed the rest of the apple into the garbage.

Roland came in and sat with us, his face relaxed, the most like a kid's since I'd met him.

"How you like Blane's new face?" he asked me. "You shoulda seen how bad he thought he was till Daddy knocked him."

"Saved your little ass," Blane said. "Pour me some coffee."

Roland poured Blane a cup and handed it to him.

"Blane told you what Bonnie did?" Roland asked. "Too bad she didn't kill that bastard."

Blane sipped his coffee and stared at the wall like he hadn't heard Roland. He had lit a cigarette, but it was already halfway burned in the ashtray and he hadn't touched it.

"Why'd she go to the hospital with him?" I asked.

Blane looked at me from the corner of his eye as though I'd asked the most ridiculous question.

"Cause he's our daddy," he said.

••

"How are your hands?" my mother asked. It was before school three days later. She hadn't said anything about the Ledets since I had punched the wall. I held out my bruised knuckles. She laughed.

"You better be glad your daddy didn't see you trying to knock a hole in his garage."

"Thanks for not telling," I said.

"I'm going job hunting today," she said. "Being around this house all the time's making me crazy."

"You look pretty," I said, and she gave me a smile. "Daddy knows you're looking for a job?"

"We talked about it last night. I guess that's why he's

still asleep, I kept him up so late." She lifted her coffee cup with both hands, blew on it and sipped. "He starts days soon, and me and you haven't even gone out for a milkshake." She sat back. "Have you seen Bonnie?"

The previous morning the Ledets' door had been ajar. I eased inside and called out, but my voice rang through the house and died without answer. I went down the hall and stopped at her father's room, the morning light harsh through the uncurtained windows, the smell of his clothes still heavy, then crossed to Bonnie's room. I knelt on the floor and searched, hoping to find something, a button, a string, a bit of her hair. Every trace had been swept clean.

"She hasn't been home," I said.

My mother waited for more, then nodded. "It's confusing sometimes, isn't it?" She forced a smile, then stared at the table. I wanted to tell her about Bonnie, about all that had happened and all that I knew, but my mother kept staring at the table, her eyes too wide. I downed my juice.

"I've gotta go," I said and stood.

"I could drive you," she said.

# Free Fall

His whole life Jimmy Strawhorn has seen the state capitol building standing like a lighthouse by the Mississippi, but never before has he set foot inside. Now each floor higher presses the elevator walls closer. He urges the elevator to hurry, swallows hard. What if he reached the capitol observation deck twenty-four floors up and the impulse came on him as strong as yesterday? Fear snags in his throat. Thirty hours ago he jumped from a sixth-story window, bounced off an awning and landed on the concrete below. He wishes he were home in his scuba gear, skirting the bottom of his plastic pool, but he knows he needs to do something. Today at work men he didn't even know stuck their heads inside the chemical tank where he was welding and called out Geronimo! Yesterday the police suggested counseling. He feels as sane as anyone.

Jimmy forces a yawn to pop his ears. The elevator groans to a stop. He listens, fearing the drop and coil of cables in the shaft below. The door slides open. Jimmy squints at the afternoon sunshine, steps without thinking to the center of the room. Tall windows surround him. The slight tremor of the building travels up his legs, through his groin, pauses for a moment in his gut, then whooshes skyward, opening the top of his head like a hatch. His sight pulses, then locks on a vision of a woman sitting behind a glass counter, her cream-colored face half covered by cobalt-blue goggles, a hard beam of sunlight setting her blond hair afire. His eyesight swims. He reaches out, stumbles, his knees rubbery. The woman stands, moves around a counter on which, he now sees, sit newspapers whose front pages tell the story of his leap. She glides toward him, her blouse a galaxy of yellow polka dots on blue, then she has his arm, her touch solid. "You all right?" she asks. He points down. She leads him inside the elevator, pushes a button. When she removes the goggles, her eyes are wide and gray. Jimmy lays his palm against her cheek. She laughs. "I'm real," she says. The elevator falls. For a moment yesterday's exhilaration is back, but the space around him is too small. He strains to focus on the descending numbers above the door, but his lungs deflate. The woman takes both his hands and smiles.

"You're scared of heights," she says. "You're not the first to come up here trying to face down their fear. My name's Sandra."

Jimmy sorts the words coming fast at him. He sees white, as though he's stood up too quickly, then he is slowing, the door opening. Sandra leads him across a marble floor. Their footsteps echo, statues loom against the walls. Mausoleum, Jimmy thinks, but Sandra says, "You're fine now," then seats him on a bench.

"I'm spinning," Jimmy says.

"Acrophobia," she says. "Fear of heights. I'm just the opposite. Fear of getting down. Good thing I'm not a duck." She laughs again. "I run the newspaper and souvenir stand. I was getting my end-of-the-day sun when I saw you."

He touches the goggles hanging around her neck. "What are these?"

"I wear them early in the morning and late in the afternoon. They're supposed to intensify the positive energy from the sun, a sort of antidepressant. It's just an idea I have."

"I'm Jimmy Strawhorn," he says.

"Jimmy Strawhorn." She furrows her brow, taps her chin. Huge chandeliers hang above him. Vertigo corkscrews through his head.

"It's an incredible place," Sandra says. "Marble from all over. It's like travelling without ever having to leave."

"I need to get outside," Jimmy says. They stand and walk, push through the heavy glass-and-brass door. For a moment Jimmy's front brushes her back, then they step out onto the broad high steps that lead to the parking lot below. Jimmy squints, thinking for a second he sees the Delta Hotel's reflective sides in the distance.

"Jimmy Strawhorn!" she says, pointing. "The one that jumped. I can't believe it. I've been reading about you all day." She pauses, lays both hands on her goggles. "You weren't coming up to . . ."

"Uh uh," he says. "I'm not crazy."

"I didn't say you were. People buying papers did, but not me. I mean, you aimed for that awning, didn't you?"

Jimmy nods.

"Let me see your hand," she says. She turns his palm upward and traces his sooty lifeline with a finger. "Good," she says. "Long and strong." Her touch spreads through him, settles like water into sand. Jimmy leans toward her.

"I'm a welder," he says.

"Why you smell like raincoats?"

"Vinyl chloride. I work inside chemical tanks."

She touches his cheek. "Your color's coming back. You're still pale, though."

"Inside of those tanks don't get much sun."

She releases his hand. Jimmy's skin strains after her, already missing her. How long since a woman touched him? Since Wendy? A year, two? Sandra studies him, her eyebrows tilted toward one another. A spark arcs between them.

"Come with me," he says. She steps back. "I mean to dinner. A thanks for helping me out."

"I don't know."

"Look, I know you don't know me. I'd really like to show my appreciation, though."

She gazes upward over her shoulder. "The stand doesn't close for ten minutes."

"I'll wait."

She drums on the goggles, squints in the direction of the Delta. "You swear you weren't coming up to jump? No awning's going to help you here."

"I swear. I had to see something."

She inhales deeply, her arms to her sides like a diver.

"Let's go now, then," she says. "I don't mind going to your place if you want to get cleaned up."

"What about the stand?"

"It'll keep. I lock the register after every customer."

She smiles once more, her face stretched tight. Jimmy's stomach rises. He feels as he has lately inside the tanks, as if he must run for air or be closed in forever. He points to the parking lot.

"I'm right down there."

••

In the car Sandra talks about the tourist sites of Louisiana, the assassination of Huey Long, the construction of the capitol, information from the books she sells at the souvenir stand. At first Jimmy follows her, but then her voice speeds with excitement, hopping from topic to topic, drawing connections he cannot follow until he listens only to her voice, washing over him, carrying him weightless on a current. He drifts, returns to where he does not want to go, two hours earlier, crouched inside a chemical tank, acetylene fumes fat in his nostrils. His torch hissed like a leak from a giant balloon. A slug of sweat inched down his spine. His bruised shoulder throbbed. Before him, his weld glowed like an evil eye, moved toward him. He threw off his mask and stood, the air ragged and rusty. The curve of the tank closed in. He dropped his torch and scrambled up the ladder.

"A lot of scientists believe those locks upriver can't hold the Mississippi," Sandra says. "They think it has to change course and go through the Atchafalaya. Some days when I'm watching the river I think about that happening, a big wave coming downstream tossing ships like sticks, rocking the bridge right off its legs, sloshing water over the levee into downtown. Then the water falling, sinking faster and faster until there's nothing but a huge ditch." She shakes her head at Jimmy. "It sends a shiver through me."

"Here we are," Jimmy says, pulling into his driveway. They step from the car and walk side by side to the door, but when they enter the house Jimmy hesitates. He had forgotten the months since anyone came here, the last the assembly man from the pool place over a year ago. Now he sees the recliner, his lone piece of furniture, and the three-foot TV screen as signs—a hermit's house. He wants to pull Sandra out, slam the door and bolt, but she walks straight to the wall covered with photos of exotic sea creatures and offshore oil platforms, touches with her fingertips the picture of an orange-suited diver suspended among fish. "This you?" she asks.

"No." His forehead tingles. "Let's go see my pool."

The four-foot-tall pool fills the backyard. From the water rises a section of pipe like an oil rig's amputated leg. Beneath the surface, valves and steel grating form a labyrinth.

"You weld underwater?" she asks.

"I'm learning. I use scuba gear, but I've never gotten certified. I'd like to work in the gulf."

"Why don't you then?" she asks. He shrugs. Sandra cups water and spreads it over her face. She tilts her head and runs her palm down her neck. "I've never been to the coast. Maybe one day you could teach me how to dive there."

He nods, but he is thinking of the things that could go wrong, panic at one hundred feet, an air tank gone empty. He doesn't even know her. His mouth goes dry. Reckless endangerment. Maybe the police were right.

"Get showered," Sandra says. "We're going to have fun."

In the bathroom Jimmy strains to hear Sandra moving about his house, but inside the cubicle of his shower, he hears nothing but his own breathing, smells the faint odor of chemicals still coating his skin. He twists both faucet handles full blast, then raises the shower lever, releasing a spray whose hiss reminds him for a second of his torch. What does she want? What is she doing now? Rummaging through his things, sneaking away to catch a taxi, wishing she wasn't here? It's been so long that he barely remembers what it is like to have a woman in his house, not even Wendy.

Jimmy presses against his eyes. Wendy. Her name is strange in his head. He'd known she was the one from the moment he met her at a friend's. Still he'd taken it slowly, calling her several times before asking her out, then taking her out several times before kissing her. They were both shy, and Jimmy liked sitting quietly with her, no pressure to make jokes, to talk small, to please her. After two months she asked him to dinner at her apartment, candlelight, wine, and soft country music, the air charged like neon. They had never done more than kiss, but at the table her low-cut dress and flowery aroma made him want to carry her to her room, lie down with her, touch her everywhere there was to touch. In his throat a spring began to coil, making it hard to swallow, even harder to think. A rushing sound swelled in his ears, his tongue thickened, his palms burned. He'd felt desire before, but never like this, not a compulsion so strong he wanted either to step away from himself for relief or to grab Wendy and fall into her, let himself go, blend with her. Wendy smiled at him, her sweet smell lingering in his nostrils. He gripped the table. The floor dropped from beneath him. He plummeted. Jimmy braced, not knowing how this sort of fall would end, braced, a void rushing past him, braced until Wendy spoke his name, leaned over and placed her hand on his shoulder, slowing him, stopping him. He shot from his chair, apologized as he headed for the door, arrived at home before the ground had steadied. He called her and told her not to worry, not to be mad or to cry, at least he thought he'd told her because after he'd hung up he wasn't sure what he'd said. No matter. He loved her. Nothing was wrong but the timing. Why leap into something so important? Better to plan, to be sure, to wait for the right time.

He began his plans, cataloguing what he needed before he could ask her to marry him. For his house he picked out appliances and new bathroom fixtures, furniture, and carpet. He decided on a new car and a boat, estimated the cost of sodding the yard and planting trees, diagrammed construction of a redwood fence and a deck, chose different paint for the bedroom, considered adding a Jacuzzi, maybe even a swing. He totalled it, figuring too how much they would need for a Hawaiian honeymoon, but he didn't tell her. Instead, he collected overtime, fourteen hours a day, six sometimes seven days a week. He begged off on dates because of fatigue, avoided going to her house because he needed to get a good night's sleep for work. When out of the blue she said it was over, he was too tired to call her back, then too tired to leave his house. No need. He had beaucoup money saved.

Months later he took work at another plant, maintenance, and before long he was planning again, not thinking of Wendy at all, scheming this time to work offshore. He read books about undersea welding, subscribed to diving magazines, bought gear and a pool. Days, he welded inside tanks, a single bulb illuminating the steel egg around him. Nights, sometimes all night, he spent in the water. Soon, he'd get certified, get on with a company offshore. Soon.

Jimmy's chest constricts the way it has lately before he leaves for work. He holds his face close to the stinging spray. And what he thinks strange is not that he is isolated but that he hasn't until this moment thought that he was isolated.

Jimmy raises his arm to lather himself and grunts, his right shoulder swollen, blue and yellow. Yesterday, because he was back on his feet so fast, he hadn't even known he'd landed. He stood there, his ears ringing, his sight thrown into clarity so penetrating that he saw the astonished mouth of a woman passing on the interstate, saw the tiny glint of a jet miles distant, saw the clouds curving toward the horizon. Closer to him, he noticed the blinding chrome and iridescent gleam of parked cars, noticed the watery grain of the concrete at his feet. Someone took his arm and sat him on the edge of the sidewalk. A young man leaned over, passed his hand back and forth before Jimmy's face. "You tripping?" the man asked. "You think you a goddamn cartoon?" The adrenaline rushed to Jimmy's brain, settled there clear and calm. Later, at home, he began to shake, fear finally catching him, but when the shakes were gone, the calm remained, shallower by degrees, until this afternoon when staring into the weld the tank had pressed in on him.

It is quiet when he emerges from the bathroom. He hurries to the backyard where Sandra sits on the edge of the pool, her feet dangling in the water, the goggles on her face even though it is twilight. She looks him over, her energy replaced by a slight heaviness. He touches his wet hair, tugs at his shirtsleeves. This is all a mistake, he thinks.

••

During dinner Jimmy talks about red snapper and manta rays in the gulf, about thirty-foot ground swells in the North Sea, about invisible winds on the ocean floor. In his mind he floats, lemon fish brushing past him, filtered light shimmering off their skin. He savors the last bite of his enchilada, swallows and touches his stomach, still hungry, then snaps to as if the room has appeared around him. Sandra stabs at the flauta she has barely touched and sets her fork on the plate.

"I've been gabbing too much," Jimmy says.

"No you haven't," she says. "I wanted to hear about you." She runs her finger around her marguerita glass, touches it to her tongue. "Why don't you work offshore?" she asks.

"I don't know enough yet."

"The stuff in your pool seemed good."

He rolls his shoulder, pops his neck.

"It's different in the sea."

She thumps the edge of her glass. "You're hiding, Jimmy Strawhorn. You talk about everything that isn't."

"They're plans."

"I saw your house. You don't ever have anybody over. I doubt you go out either. You ever taken a diving class?"

The distance between them expands and contracts. Jimmy searches her eyes for something to tell him she's making generalizations, like an astrology chart or a fortune cookie, but her eyes are certain.

"You're nothing but mysteries," she says. "You jumped out a building and all you can talk about is fish. You're not here."

He goes back to the moment, poised on the windowsill, the sun full in his face, his shoulders tense.

"I'm here," he says. "How come you are?"

She points at him. "Do you believe in omens? What do you think the chances were we'd meet today, the day after you jumped, the day I read about you in the paper? When's the last time you went up in the capitol?"

The skin on the back of his neck bunches. "Never."

"See? Something's happening here. When you walked in all dazed and then just stared at me, I knew you were the one who was going to take me down."

"Take you down?"

"From up there." She leans forward. "Tell me something you don't want to tell."

"Like what?"

"Something secret. A habit or a crime. Something personal."

It is all crazy, but he can't say it is crazy. He is a man who checked into a hotel and jumped six stories. The instant before he fell the world came clear before him. He pictured the road running south, across the Pontchartrain, into the swamp, all the way to the gulf, its water sparkling with sunshine diamonds.

"I didn't leave my house for four months," he says.

"Why?" Sandra touches his hand. Her fingernails are chewed to the quick.

"I got jilted."

"And?"

"And I stayed in my house."

"And you got your pool and all that underwater stuff, right?" Jimmy moves his hand from hers. "Tell all of it," she says. "Why'd she jilt you?"

He shrugs, but sweat is rising on his skin. "I got caught up in things. We were only together a while. For a long time I didn't even ask her to my place."

Sandra nods. "You were scared."

"What?" he asks.

"Do you still love her?"

He tries again to picture Wendy, but her face is vague, as if underwater. He inhales, a hand closing on his lungs.

"I'm not sure." He shifts in his seat. "Is that strange?"

"Everything is strange. Everything is normal, too."

Sandra's face opens to him. He tries to blend strange and normal, tries to make normal his leap from the Delta, his staying at home, his being here with Sandra, but all of it is strange, his whole life foreign and speeding away from him toward a place he's never imagined.

"Put your palm to my palm," she says. He raises his hand to hers, fingertips, thumbtips, palms. "Are you nervous?" she asks.

"Yes. Why don't you tell a secret?" he says.

"You won't like it. It's all coming together."

"Tell me."

She takes her hand from his, pours salt into her palm, shifts the grains, then brushes them away. "Something went wrong with my husband. That's why I came to Baton Rouge."

"Went wrong?"

"He made me quit my job. He wouldn't let me leave the house without him." Sandra clinks her knife and fork together, then lays them in an X. When she looks at him again, gravity has settled on her.

"Billy took to spying on me. He ran off all my friends, said we were plotting against him. Then he gave away our TV so I'd have to sit in the bedroom with him real quiet at night, listening to see if anybody was outside. It was creepy."

"Keep going."

"He just got weirder, so after a while I started taking a dollar from his wallet, saving and saving until I had enough for a bus ticket. Only problem was I didn't know where to go. I was scared, too. Then one day I heard that song on the radio, 'Me and Bobby McGee,' where Janis is in Baton Rouge. I packed a suitcase and called a cab and when the bus took off I was humming and feeling great."

Sandra holds her palm over the candle in the center of the table, shadowing her face. When she jerks her hand away, the flame ignites in her eyes.

"What else?" Jimmy says. "I want to hear."

"You know how it is, how you get used to something

even when it's bad. That's a long ride from north Louisiana to Baton Rouge. I started thinking about the city, how I'd never been, not even to Little Rock. I pictured all those city people gone crazy like Billy, and all those streets I didn't know the names of, all of it so big. I had to go to the toilet and be sick. When I came out, I felt even lower, and then I started thinking of Billy when he found me gone, how he wouldn't be sad but mad, furious, and how he'd wreck everything and wish I was there so he could take it out on me.

"When I finally got to the station in Baton Rouge, I left my bag and walked out and the first thing I saw was the capitol building, going way up, higher than any building I'd ever seen. Huge. I started walking toward it, watching it get higher and higher against the sky, above everything. I wanted to go to the top where I could look out and see all those miles, but then I thought no matter how far I saw, how long I looked, I wouldn't know anybody anywhere." Sandra picks up the candle, moves it close to her face and stares into it. The small fire plays on her eyes. "I felt even more by myself than I had with Billy. I wanted to get to the top as quick as I could."

The air leaves Jimmy, the same as the moment he dropped from the ledge. He looks at Sandra's face, the candlelight burning on her cheeks. "I told you you wouldn't like it," she says.

"You were going to jump."

"But I didn't. You did."

"Not like that. I didn't want to die."

"Then take me to the hotel. I have to go there."

"Why?"

"I'm not sure. I just know something brought you to the capitol. We've got to go full circle."

Jimmy shakes his head. "I can't."

"You have to. I came here. I didn't know what would happen, what you might do, but I came. Fate sent you to me, Jimmy Strawhorn. I have to know why."

••

While Sandra rents the room, Jimmy sits in the dark parking lot, rubbing his hands. He doesn't think that she wants to kill herself, but he can't know for sure. All he knows is that today he was trapped again inside a hole, alone until he met Sandra. Now his life is tumbling, at least towards somewhere. Maybe she is right. Maybe fate has brought them together.

Nearby, the awning that broke Jimmy's fall has been reanchored and reinforced. His eyes climb the hotel, window by window, until he reaches the one from which he fell. Yesterday the window had been on fire, the sun trapped within its single frame. Every morning he had driven the same route to work but never before yesterday had he seen the window blazing as if the sun itself were caught inside the room. Jimmy had stared. The car's ceiling sagged, the air bulged with heat and seared steel. Suffocating. He'd swerved onto the exit, sped through a caution light and slid into the Delta's parking lot.

"You okay?" Sandra says, startling him. She leans through the car window, the room key dangling from her finger. "Ready to go?"

Jimmy tugs his welder's cap down near his eyes and steps out. Sandra takes his hand. Through the glass doors light spills toward them. In the lobby Jimmy walks behind Sandra, his shoulders hunched, his head lowered to disguise himself. He does not remember walking this way before, does not remember what he was thinking, realizes that there had been no thoughts, only a thrumming in his head and a tunnel collapsing behind him. In the elevator Sandra squeezes his arm to her side, and he must inhale to ward off the feeling that his whole body is being squeezed. "Hold on," Sandra says. Jimmy concentrates on the warmth of her body against his. He thinks for the first time that maybe she wants to make love, a possibility that tightens his lungs and floats spots across his eyes. He tries to remember Wendy, her lips and her taste, but the blank he draws is total. Had he even touched her once his plans began?

The elevator slows to a stop and opens, but Jimmy feels himself still rising, releases Sandra's arm and steps from the elevator. The hall tilts like a chute. Sandra walks past him to the room from yesterday, unlocks the door, shoves it open and waits. Jimmy steadies himself with a hand on the wall, then hurries past Sandra. The window is a pale crack between curtains. He feels the door close behind him. "Leave it dark," Jimmy says. He tugs the fingers of one hand with the other.

"Yesterday, what were you thinking?" Sandra asks.

"Nothing. I can't remember thinking at all." Fear lands flat in his stomach. Claustrophobia rings off the walls coaxing him ever so slightly towards the window. He walks across the carpeted floor, slides open the curtains and undoes the latch. He raises the window, feels the outside pull at him.

"Talk to me," Sandra says, close behind him. "Tell me how it is."

The warm, sticky breeze slips across Jimmy's face. "Come next to me," he says. "Hold your hands out the window. Close your eyes." He feels himself lean toward the outside, feels Sandra's shoulder touch his like a tiny shock. "Can you feel it? The space pulling you?"

"I think so. A part of my head is sort of bending."

"It's like everything is reaching out and pulling. Do you feel it?"

Jimmy looks at Sandra standing like a sleepwalker, her arms out before her, her blond hair held from her shoulders by the breeze. His hand raises to touch her, but vertigo twists him in its funnel, urges him toward the outside. Sandra takes his arm and peers down to where Jimmy knows the awning is a small blue square.

"You really didn't want to kill yourself," she says.

"I didn't want to. I didn't not want to either. I just came up here. I had to."

"Tell me how you did it. Exactly how." Sandra's eyes glisten with the illumination of the city. Jimmy follows the lights outside to the edge of where he can see.

"I know how awnings are anchored in walls. I guess I knew it would break my fall if I hit it dead center, I guess something in me knew. I asked for a room on the fourth, fifth, or sixth floor over the front door and came straight in and opened the window. I swung one leg over the window ledge and then the other and I just sat. The sun was warm on me and there was that morning smell, kind of damp but crisp. I wasn't scared, I felt totally calm, but I also felt like, like everything out there was swirling through me. Know what I mean?"

Sandra squeezes his arm again, but he does not look at her. In his head he is on the ledge, on it more clearly now than the day before.

"I only stayed for a second, then I dropped off. I didn't push, I just dropped and twisted and laid flat back. Then I was laying still and the building was shooting out of the ground, except I was getting heavier, going faster, and that's when it flashed I was scared of heights. I said, 'Ha!,' just like that, 'Ha!'" Jimmy sways, widens his footing for balance.

"What happened when you hit?"

"Everything jolted and went white for a second, like somebody'd hit me with the broad side of a paddle, then I was flouncing, going a lot slower. I don't remember land-ing in the parking lot. Next thing I knew every-thing around me was bright and clear, like when I don't remember the daylight before I flip my welder's mask."

For a second Jimmy flies out over the city. He steps

back. Behind him, Sandra walks over and sits on the bed. In the poor light her face has no features.

"Come here," she says. Jimmy sits on the mattress beside her.

"How'd you get this room again?" he asks.

"I told the boy at the desk I wanted the one where the man jumped from. He smiled and gave it to me."

Jimmy glances over her pale face, hesitates, opens his mouth to hers when she leans toward him. Her warm lips and dry tongue brighten him. A door in his chest opens to her chest, opens so wide that when she sits back from him, a vacuum seems to fill him. The room hums, the traffic on the interstate sounding through the window like distant surf. The emptiness outside snakes in like the tail of a twister. Sandra looks away.

"Every day at the souvenir shop I talk to people from other places about where they've been and where they're going," Sandra says. "I picture those places in my head. I look out and see the Mississippi winding off into the distance, and I think of myself riding that water north to Missouri and Ohio or south to the gulf, on to Mexico or Europe. I used to like that, going in my head. But not now. I've never really been anywhere."

Sandra brushes her fingers across his cheek, through the hair above his ear, down behind his head. Jimmy shuts his eyes. In his mind the trail her fingers have traced glows like phosphorous. Her smell fills him. Together they lie back on the bed. Jimmy's tired body relaxes, tension and soreness moving in waves from him. Sandra sits up and stares toward the window.

"After Billy got strange, he used to take me out in the woods, to wilderness, my heart beating ninety to nothing, until we found a place he thought was right, pretty or safe or whatever. Then we'd spread a blanket and take out a bottle of bourbon and just sit, listening. When it got dark, he would ask me to take my clothes off and he'd do it, too, and then we'd paint each other with this camouflage, touching each other like we used to, real gentle. Sometimes it scared me so bad thinking what he might be fixing to do I wanted to run away, but I still think about it."

She takes Jimmy's face in her hands, her fingernails jagged against his skin. She kisses him hard, a kiss that crashes through him and makes him kiss her back, press his body against hers. He wants to be with her, take her with him to the coast, swim out into the salt night, go with her as far as she wants to go. Sandra stands, touches his face from above, then walks to the window.

"Sandra?" he says.

"I kept reading the story about you over and over, all day, Jimmy," she says. "Everybody who bought a paper talked about it, most of them saying you couldn't even kill yourself right or calling you crazy, but I told them if you were really crazy you would've jumped from higher. I kept on thinking about what made you do it, kept going out on the observation deck and trying to imagine how it would be to fall. But none of it came close to what you told me. And I swear I was wishing I could talk to you when you walked off the elevator."

Jimmy puts his feet on the floor. The city light sharpens Sandra's silhouette. His eyes trace the line of her nose, sort the ends of her hair, follow the smooth round-ness of her shoulder, his vision in the dim light as clear and sharp as in the parking lot yesterday. He starts to go to her, but she faces him.

"People ask me out all the time," Sandra says, "but I've been careful. You see, that first day, when I got to the top of the capitol, I started feeling safe, away from Billy, above it all like that. Now I work there every day. Every day. I've got a safe place like what most people want and never find, but then I go out on the observation deck and I look down where people are specks and cars are toys and I think, you know, the safest place is death. That's what safety is. I don't want that."

Jimmy stands, the distance between him and Sandra farther than a leap. The wind lifts the curtains from the window and curls them around her sides.

"I want to be with you, Jimmy," she says, and before Jimmy can move, she is gone out into the night.

He runs, in slow motion like movement through liquid, toward the window, straining, listening, time like falling time, suspended, his hands outstretched. He hears the heavy twang of the awning's metal, feels his feet one after the other dragging, the night opening, his body scattering, the feeling once more of free fall.

He jams his palms against the sill, stops himself halfway out and looks down.

On the awning below, Sandra lies still, her limbs spread, her blond hair fanned out. Jimmy sees her face close to his, as if their lips are about to touch. Her presence pulls him. "Sandra!" he says, not loudly, but the sound carries, his voice, her name, travelling. "Sandra!" he says.

She raises her hand and waves.

# Exterminator

Bob steered into the parking lot going faster than he wanted, his truck skidding on gravel before he could slow. He hadn't seen Tricia in two years, since just after he had moved out, hadn't spoken to her either until a half hour ago when she called him as he was leaving for work, her sixth sense telling her the exact moment he was walking out the door. In front of the convenience store, Tricia stared, her arms crossed. From this distance she looked the same as when they had met eleven years before—mop-top hair streaked blond and brown, dark-leather tan, hard horseback-rider's body. When Bob stepped from the truck, he felt as if she had punched her fist through his chest and was slowly opening her fingers inside.

"Sorry I called like this," she said. "Hope I'm not making you late for work." Her eyes were bloodshot, the skin at their corners drawn. She had on heavy makeup, unlike her natural look when they had been together. He hesitated to move closer, the anger and attraction already alive in him again. When she stepped nearer, he saw the bruise on her jaw.

"What's the matter?" he said.

"I knew you'd be mad."

"What would you be? This is kinda sudden."

She glanced both ways down the road. "Let's sit in my car."

Lately there had been whole days when Bob hadn't thought of her. Now in the passenger seat the familiar smells of their past swarmed him—Dr. Peppers, Benson and Hedges menthols, the sweetness of marijuana. The Mardi Gras beads they caught their last year together no longer hung from the mirror. On the dashboard lay a foldover matchbook from Red Stick Welding, the place her boyfriend worked. Bob rubbed his chin. How many times had that bastard been in this seat?

"Rick hit you?" he asked.

Tricia's eyes widened. She thumped a cigarette from her pack and lit it. She touched the bruise, flicked her cigarette hard.

"I shouldn't have called. I've been up all night. He was going crazy, said if I tried to leave he'd kill me."

"I told you not to get mixed up with that bastard."

"You told me you'd hurt anybody I got mixed up with. You don't even know him."

"He's a goddamn Nazi."

"He's Dutch."

A month after Bob had moved out, he dropped by the trailer and found Rick in a bikini bathing suit, washing Tricia's car. Bob wanted to kick his ass then, but Tricia made him leave.

"I was messed up then," Bob said. "I'm better now."

Tricia took a deep drag, tilted her head back exposing the curve of her throat. "Maybe you were right. He always had a temper. Now he's mad all the time, raving about how stupid Americans are. Last night Desert Storm on TV set him off."

"Let him take his ass back to Europe then."

"He kept saying, 'Fuck the army.'" She smiled. "It reminded me of you."

Tricia's hazel eyes sparked green. Her fingers spread wider in him. Bob picked up Rick's matches, glanced around the rest of the car. "What do you want?" he asked.

"To talk. Rick's chased everybody I know off."

"He hit you before?"

She nodded. "I told him to move out a month ago. He said he'd kill me and be in Central America before anybody even knew."

"He's serious?"

"He's crazy. I called the sheriff's office. They were a lot of help. They told me I had to give him a week to get out if I evicted him. I did that, he'd burn the place."

"So you want me to run him off?"

"No, that's not what I want. You hear me?" She ground out her cigarette. "Shit, this was a mistake."

"I ain't out of line. You called me."

"I don't want that, Bob. I mean it."

Her expression blazed, the fear replaced by the defiance that had made Bob fall for her in the first place. Even now he had to hold himself back, the link between them almost chemical. Worse, unfinished business sucked at him. He looked away. On a telephone pole, a large yellow bow shone in the sun.

"This is a lot to take in, you know," he said. "I don't hear from you in ages and now you call out of nowhere."

"I said I was sorry. Why don't we talk about something else." She pointed at the "Willie's Extermination" patch on his shirt. "How long you had this job?"

"A few months. I quit my last job, I didn't get fired."

"Did I say you got fired?" She took out another cigarette. "Are you like that Robocop guy on the commercial?"

"Boy, never heard that one. I'm taking the certification test in a couple of weeks. You still filling card racks?"

"Six days a week. The war's got business way up."

"The war. What bullshit. Fucking oil companies."

She looked at him, then laid her head back and smiled. "Remember that night we were tripping on Scenic Highway by Exxon and you started yelling out the window they were burning up the world?" She poked her tongue against her lip and brushed at her forehead as if something had lighted there. He couldn't remember ever seeing her scared, not even during the fights of their final year, not even after she punched him and he pushed her down. His hands went cold. She had complained about his temper, but he had never hit her. She glanced at her watch, then side to side.

"I've got to go," she said.

"Go? I just got here."

"I need to get to work. I've got four Wal-Marts today."

"So what? You can't rush me out here and then take off. You afraid he's gonna see us?"

"Maybe. He follows me sometimes."

"I wish he'd followed you. Tell me what you want."

"I said to talk. I need to get my balance."

"You need to get rid of that prick. We need to talk about that."

"No. We don't."

In the store window their reflections sat side by side just like the old days. She used to drive fast, and Bob had loved to ride with her, smoking a joint, the Animals or Zeppelin coursing through him. Even during the worst times, Tricia seemed to be speeding them away from their problems.

"I don't want you in trouble over this," she said. "You're the only one I can tell. Can you listen?"

"You gonna be all right?"

"Yeah. I need to go, though."

"You'll call me?"

"When I can."

••

Bob took the knife from his belt and pried at the lid on a can of Baygon. He was purposely not looking at his coworker, Mann, who leaned against the pickup, eating a candy bar.

"Describe a black widow bite," Mann said.

"I told you stop quizzing me," Bob said.

"How you find termites?"

"I know the test."

Mann glanced through the window of Bob's truck. "What's the difference between a roof rat and a Norway rat?"

Bob wondered sometimes if the reason he hadn't slapped Mann was because Willie was his daddy, but he knew the real reason was a slap would only rattle the beans in Mann's head. Mann popped the last bite of candy into his mouth and licked his fingers. Bob knew Mann hadn't washed his hands after spraying, but then that was nothing. The shit he had seen that idiot and Willie do with poison boggled the mind. Just last week Willie had unscrewed a clogged hose from a full sprayer and blown on it like a trumpet. Bob pictured tumors hanging like clusters of grapes inside them.

"You're a roof rat," Bob said. "A turd-eating roof rat."

"And you're a pussy. You can't kill nothing. This morning I ran over a squirrel just for the hell of it." Mann grinned.

Bob knew Mann wasn't joking. Mann himself was the joke, an exterminator who loved to kill, especially when it would piss Bob off. Mann was constantly putting some carcass, a possum or a cat or a raccoon, in the bed of Bob's truck even though Bob had already threatened him. Once Mann even came in bragging how he'd lawnmowered two frogs humping in his yard.

"You're a sick fuck," Bob said.

"No, I'm a professional. You're scared of it. You're

scared of the chemicals and you're scared to kill anything except a little bug or a rat."

Bob stood and looked Mann in the eye.

"How'd you get named Mann? You can't even spell
it right."

"Don't slam my name, bro."

"Get away from my truck."

"Your truck. Eat me," Mann said, spun and walked
inside.

Bob touched the rim of his eye, hoping more dirt
hadn't gotten inside his contact. That would be the last
downswing on the seesaw this day had been, up with
the excitement of seeing Tricia, down with the worry
over what was happening to her. Luckily today's clients
had been people he liked, people he was glad to help
clean the vermin out of their houses, all except the last,
a woman with years of dog shit scattered through her
house and who bitched about why Bob couldn't kill her
roaches. Today he'd had to crawl under her bathroom
through a puddle of leaky sewage to chop a two-foot
copperhead. Still that wasn't as bad as some, like at Mall
City, the crackhead apartment complexes where he had
seen two shootings, or the house of the unbathed sur-
vivalist who rack-racked killing everybody from abor-
tionists to football coaches. Sometimes it seemed like
the people Bob tried to help were nastier than the
things he killed.

Bob locked the tool case on the truck and walked inside where Willie and Mann were watching the war on TV. Above Willie's desk hung the company motto: Infestation Everywhere. On screen, soldiers shoved a round into an artillery piece and fired.

"One raghead grease-job coming up," Mann said.

Bob hadn't turned on the war news the last few days, but everywhere he went it surrounded him. Sane, mild-mannered people casually discussed murdering Saddam Hussein, revelled in the slaughter of Iraqis, marvelled at death technology, all of them locked to their TVs, waiting for the next violent image. Some tried to deny the real reason they were watching by saying they wanted to see what the government was up to or saying they wanted to know what was happening to the troops, but they were still aflame with war fever, caught in the thrill of it. As if they'd ever raised and fired, ever seen bits of skull fly like broken ceramic.

"I'm outta here," Bob said.

"What's the matter," Mann asked, "can't stand to see a bunch of sand niggers get theirs?"

Bob bit the inside of his lip, turned and shoved out the door. Outside he stopped, shut his eyes and breathed slowly until he levelled. In his truck the *Exterminator's Handbook* lay open on the seat: "Roof Rat (*Rattus rattus*): pointed nose, light slender haunch. Norway Rat (*Rattus norvegicus*): blunt nose, heavy thick haunch." Bob flipped the book closed.

On the way home he splurged for some boiled shrimp and kept his windows rolled up to hold in the smell. In his apartment he spilled them onto a plate, held it close to his nose and inhaled, the peppery aroma spreading into his forehead. He thought of Tricia's salty skin, the reddish tips of her hair after a day in the sun, thought of beer so icy its taste came only after you'd swallowed. He settled into the chair next to his water bed and turned on CNN. A man on TV demonstrated Iraqi entrenchment—fiery moats, trenches, tunnels. Animation of a buried tank appeared. Its turret, pulsing red with heat from the day's sun, protruded from the sand. Heat-sensing jets were blowing them away. *For every roach you see, there are fifty more you don't.* Bob lifted one of the shrimp, studied its tiny legs and antennae, its translucent skin. He dropped it back onto the plate.

With the remote he killed the picture. He popped open a can of beer, poured half the contents down his throat, swallowed and tugged at his lips. From this spot he could see his entire apartment—a single room. A forty-year-old man, alone and killing bugs for a living. He'd never imagined it.

He and Tricia had bought land and put a nice mobile home on it. Spur of the moment they headed out on adventures, the river bluffs at Port Hudson, the beach at Grande Isle, country cemeteries late at night. From the start it was intense, two edgy people who undestood the other's anger without understanding how to cure it. Then the fights started and the more they fought the more they partied. They blew tons of money, so much that Bob had to work overtime at Dow just to make ends meet. Endless shifts unloading tank cars, cleaning tank cars, moving tank cars, loading tank cars. A trap. They grew tired of each other's explosiveness and sullenness, talked to each other less, and the less they talked the more intense the sex became, the better then weirder then kinkier right up to the end—straps, belts, even burns. Since Tricia, Bob had slept with other women, but there had been little emotion, just Tricia's absence in bed with him, taunting. Still, lately he had been able to sit alone and not think of her, not need to be with anyone.

Bob finished his beer, loaded his bat hit and sat on the edge of his bed. After a couple of tokes, he drummed his fingers on the telephone. He wanted to call but a mysterious caller might be enough to set Rick off. But then, who knew that wasn't what Tricia wanted. Some fucked-up conflict or excuse to pop the motherfucker. Bob stripped off his clothes, checked each item for rogue insects, then flung them, shirt, socks, pants, underwear, against the wall. As steam roiled from the running water, he sat on the edge of the tub, examining his skin for bites and rashes. Checking himself was a daily ritual, but sometimes at night he still awoke thrashing, the crawl of tiny legs on him. Once he dreamed of Mann and Willie setting a grand table, goblets of poison at each plate, a giant basted worm laid on a platter. The infestation of dreams was the worst.

He eased into the tub, lay back and closed his eyes.

He saw Tricia propped on the kitchen bar, giving Rick the expression she had given Bob so often, the expression that told you how stupid you were, that ignored and insulted at the same time, that made you mad to prove her wrong and accept you again. Rick moved toward her, screamed at her, swung his fist into Tricia's face. Bob bolted upright. He tossed water into his face, stretched his eyes. He had to slow down. Be patient. His life was finally almost free of turmoil. He couldn't let it seep back in.

••

Bob set the last empty can of the six-pack onto the floor, hoping to doze in his chair, but the phone rested like a bomb beside him. He thought of moths drawn miles together by an invisible signal beyond their will, tried to laugh but saw again the bruise and fear on Tricia's face. He grabbed his keys and headed out.

By the time he turned off I-12, his buzz had sharpened into a headache. Trees and darkness crowded the winding state highway, headlights of oncoming cars pierced his temples like pincers. It was a long time since he'd been on this road, and his mind travelled ahead to the trailer. He and Tricia had made that place a home, filling and adorning it with their things, her strange melting Dali prints, his king-size water bed, the matching easy chairs in the living room. Water oaks and pines shaded their lot and on windy nights he and Tricia had lain next to an open window, the shushing and creaking of trees covering them. Once in a while they wandered into the woods without a flashlight until their eyes adjusted to a perfect spot. There they made love standing, arms and legs slick with bug repellant, one of their backs against a tree. Right now he felt her lips against his.

Bob turned onto the gravel road, cut his lights and slowed. The grind beneath his tires centered in his head, churning. He parked across the street and stared through the trees at the trailer, his and Tricia's trailer, dark except for the bedroom. It would be different inside, his belongings gone, his smell replaced by Rick's smell, his bed replaced by another bed. Rick in all the places Bob had once been. Bob's hands tightened on the steering wheel. There was Rick on top of Tricia, her body tensed and resisting, Rick's fingers clutched in her hair.

Bob banged his hands on the dash, squeezed from his throat a noise that repulsed him. His arms, his legs, then his whole body shook. Saliva filled his mouth. The old reactions. He and Tricia at the last. Silence and rage. Only sex was missing.

An image from the final months hatched full grown. One night, wasted, he had shattered a glass unicorn that Tricia's mother had given her. Laughing, he staggered off to bed and crashed. In his nightmare his skin burned, stung again and again by something in the dark. He swatted and thrashed, every movement increasing the stings, finally threw himself awake in a tangle of blankets. For a moment he was relieved to have escaped, then the burning and stinging were back, worse now, deeper and more pointed. He touched a hand to his side, jerked at the pain as if his own touch were needles. The pain spread to his butt, his legs, his back, his balls, all at once. He sat totally still, his eyesight adjusting to the weak light through the curtain. Blood shone black on his skin. Here and there on the sheet he picked out a wing, a horse's leg, a head. Light glinted off tiny quills on his skin. Glass shards. He screamed for Tricia, even though he knew she was gone, then reached for a cigarette to smoke before he made his way out of bed. As he smoked he imagined his revenge, binding and stranding her somewhere while she was tripping. When he finished his smoke, he pulled his feet up under him, stood and jumped to the floor, a few pieces driving into his soles. For hours he plucked and dug glass from himself, kept finding bits all through the day. Two days later Tricia returned, but neither of them mentioned the incident. The violence Bob had played through his head, that Tricia had in her eyes, they carried to the bedroom.

Twenty yards from Bob, the bedroom light went out. He pushed against his temples. He could kick in the door and be down the hall before the bastard was even out of bed. Bare arms and legs flinging sheets, naked bodies scrambling, Tricia screaming No! He cranked the truck and drove away.

••

Bob leaned over and pumped the can of Lindane—

five, six, seven times—a vigorous pump for each day since he'd seen Tricia. He struggled not to call, not to follow her to a job site to see how she was, but each day she didn't call, the greater his terror and anger grew. Was she hurt and unable to call? Or was she playing with his head, not telling him what she really wanted, just waiting to see where he stumbled and how long it would take him to blow? No. She had told him to wait and listen and he would. He wasn't like in the old days. He had learned. He wouldn't push and maybe they could start again, differently, with openness and an understanding of what walls between them could breed.

Bob looked out from the center of the dingy apartment. More than two dozen roaches prowled around the door frame, feeding on the butt of a sandwich left on an end table. *Infestation is not necessarily a slow process. Reproduction is often logarithmic, so an environment absolutely free of intruders can be quickly overrun.* Bob knew from the sourness in the air that the kitchen would be worse.

"Y'all seen a lot of insects?" he asked the couple, who were watching TV from the couch. On the screen, arrows showed the possible routes of allied forces flanking the Iraqis.

"We seen some," said the man. "They like to hide." The man's arms seemed a little too short for his chunky torso, his head almost mongoloid. The woman's belly swelled with an advanced pregnancy, but her shoulder bones threatened to poke through the fabric of her dress.

These were exactly the kind of people who let their house pile into a garbage heap, then called Willie to complain that their roaches weren't dead. He felt like spraying them.

"This chemical stinks pretty bad," Bob said, pulling on his mask. "It flushes 'em, too. Y'all might want to wait outside."

"We're looking at this show," the woman said. She lit another cigarette, the smoke from the last one still hovering.

Bob tucked his pants legs into his socks, fastened his shirt's top button and slipped on his gloves. He stuck the nozzle behind a velvet print of a clown and sprayed. Roaches exploded onto the wall, scurrying in every direction. Several took flight, lumbering into the air. Bob wrinkled his nose, then squirted into a crack in the door frame. From every hole and crevice roaches poured. He blasted the wall, coated the floor at his feet, ducked and let loose a stream at the ceiling. He backed away from the wall, the room aswarm with insects. From his belt he took a can of Baygon and released a misty spray, knocking roaches from the air, sending them into spasms on the floor. He spurted into a quarter-sized hole in the wall, let go a burst under a chair and behind the couch. His skin bunched, a clog rose in his throat, but he gritted his teeth.

He'd struck them where they lived and he was winning. Hundreds of the brown bugs twitched on the floor. Then he saw the couple, whom he'd forgotten, standing between the couch and the TV. Roaches buzzed the air around them, landed on their heads, but the couple stayed, swatting, staring at Bob through the cloud of insecticides. Bob stormed into the kitchen. Two plastic bags spilled garbage from their mouths across the floor. In the sink grungy dishes, pots, and pans reeked with an odor that cut through the smell of Lindane and made Bob gag. Bugs stirred by the skirmish in the den already scrambled across the walls, but when Bob sprayed both poisons at once, the place came alive. He stomped and ducked, squinted and kept on with both cans. He was using way too much poison for a living area, but he couldn't stop. These people had lost control. They were being taken over in their own apartment, were infesting other apartments. He swung open a cabinet door. A nest of inch-long Americans went airborne straight at him. He stepped back, stumbled, fell into the garbage. The bags collapsed beneath him, the green plastic ballooning on either side, spewing tin cans and chicken bones and more roaches. He scrambled to his feet, bugs on his arms and legs. He sprayed his own shirt, dropped the cans and brushed at himself. He broke from the kitchen cursing, his hands held out in front of him, jerked open the door and dashed through, still thrashing even though he was outside.

Bob knocked the last couple of roaches from his shoulder, tore off his mask and work shirt. He shook his hair, the tingle of small legs all over him, then clutched at his chest, cleared his throat and gagged.

"What the fuck is going on?" Mann asked, sauntering up. He peered around the door. "Christ! Air show!" Bob looked in at the people coughing and fanning at the roaches still in flight. A mist of spray swirled from the kitchen.

"Shit," Bob said, and spat.

"Fucking roach olympics. Hey," Mann said to the couple. "You people heard of cleaning?" The man and woman glanced at each other.

Bob trudged back in and retrieved the cans, the couple following him. He wanted to scream at them, grab them and shake them, but he brushed past.

"It makes 'em fly," the man said.

"You ain't done the bedroom," said the woman.

"We'll leave them for pets," Bob said, and shut the door.

"Think you used enough poison?" Mann said as he followed Bob to his truck.

"I should've torched the fucking place." Bob tossed his gear into the back of his truck and leaned against the side.

"What a mess," Mann said. "Goddamn white people, too."

Bob's ears rang. He pressed his hands to them.

"I'd like to take a body count in that place," Mann said. "I'll bet you stroked a thousand of those little shits."

"Hoo-fucking-ray." Bob's beeper sounded. He plopped into the driver's seat, inhaled and got Willie on the radio.

"Somebody named Tricia wants you to meet her at the Essen Lane Kmart," Willie said.

Bob squeezed the steering wheel, trying to steady himself, but the poison burned his nostrils, made him sneeze. Those people weren't right. He'd seen that, known that. The woman was pregnant, too. His eyes stung, blurred with water.

••

Bob strode toward the card section, fingering the knife on his belt and half-expecting Rick to step from an aisle. Tricia was plugging brightly colored cards into slots on a display rack, her back to him. He touched her shoulder. She started and turned. He'd dreaded seeing black eyes and a swollen lip, but her exhausted face without makeup was worse. He wanted both to hug her and to shake her.

"I been worried fucking sick," he said, his speech thick and cottony in a way he knew she recognized. "Why ain't you called?"

"I did call."

"You know what I mean. He touched you again?"

She narrowed her eyes. "He hasn't touched me. Son of a bitch better not touch me."

"You told him to get out?"

Tricia glanced toward two women watching them and closed her box of cards. "Let's get a Coke," she said, and started walking.

At the snack bar, Tricia played a rhythm on the counter as she waited for the drinks she'd ordered. She had short fingers, strong hands. For a moment Bob felt them on his face. Tricia looked from the corner of her eye.

"Bob?"

He nodded, but the wariness had already settled on her.

Tricia led him into the bright sun where they sat on the curb. Five feet away metal grating covered a drain. Bob's mind started down the hole. He forced his eyes forward.

"I been scared sick," he said. "You should've called."

"I had to figure some things out first. He hasn't hit me again. He's been quiet."

Her tone made him remember her, across the room, her eyes red from fatigue, a wavering cloud of smoke suspended in the air. Now as then, the distance between them expanded.

"He knew I'd seen you," she said. "He'll know I saw you today."

"Then let me come with you."

"No. It was stupid pulling you in. I've got to settle this myself."

"I can take care of that asshole. I won't even hurt him. I'll scare him enough to leave."

"You know you'd hurt him and you'd be in jail. Even your old cop buddies couldn't get you out of that."

"Evict him and I'll come stay till he gets out."

"Goddamnit, quit."

Bob stood. He removed the cup's plastic top to take

a gulp, but a gust of wind snatched it from his hand and sent it tumbling across the lot.

"Why'd you pull me in if you won't let me do anything?"

"I was scared. I had to talk to somebody."

"You got to give him an ultimatum."

"You think I don't know that? Last time I told him he had to go, he got his pistol out and cleaned it. You can't force me, Bob. You're still forcing."

"And you're still messing with me. You act like you want to let me in, then you lock the door."

"Yeah? Well, you think the only way through a door is a kick."

Bob sipped the Coke, syrupy and too cold. He tried to work saliva into his mouth, then wiped the corners where he knew cotton was gathering.

"I should've called back," she said.

"Yeah, you should have."

"All I wanted was to talk. Why couldn't you just talk?"

"I thought the dude was about to kill you. How was I supposed to act?"

"I don't know. I still don't know."

"Great. Ya know, you been fucking up ever since you let that shithead move in. Jesus, our sheets weren't even cold."

"They were to me."

She stood, but he put his hand on her forearm. For a second her face showed pain, then she moved her arm and looked away.

"Tricia, I love you."

"I'm sorry."

"Fuck that. You started it again. You knew what I'd want to do."

"I hoped you'd hear what I said."

"Right." Bob linked his hands behind his head. On every light pole, a yellow bow flapped in the nippy breeze. Homecoming. He tasted bitterness far back in his throat.

"Maybe I did want you to do something," Tricia said. "It wasn't fair. It's too late now, though."

"No it ain't. It would work. It could all work."

"It's not working right now."

Bob threw the rest of his drink on the ground. He crumpled the cup. "I have to see you."

"You can't. I'm too tired."

••

Bob carried his sprayer out of the kitchen and into the living area. This morning he'd passed the test, easy, a letdown really. Now he stood in the final unit of the three apartment complexes he and Mann had treated today, a neat, cozy place almost completely free of roaches. The last time he'd come here, bugs had been migrating from neighbors' apartments, but the people who lived here had used his help to keep the pests under control. It was a good feeling.

He raised his nozzle to spray behind a hanging picture, noticed the photo in the frame. A young black couple sat at a picnic table, their arms around each other, their free hands on the shoulders of a small girl before them. Bob squirted behind the picture, then with one hand lifted an end of the couch, moved it aside and dropped it. He shot a stream of poison onto the baseboard, noticed a loose corner of carpet, knelt and peeled it back. A crack at the baseboard. Residue. Termites? He visualized the wall's interior, joists riddled and teeming with white insects, wood crumbling and collapsing. He sprayed into it and stood. His head swam. He saw Tricia beneath him, her tongue on her upper lip, her eyes rolled back, her hands on his cheeks. He tossed his head, leaned against the wall, blew out through his mouth. Behind him the apartment door opened.

"Quit whackin' it, the Mann is here." Mann plopped onto the couch. Splotches of insecticide covered his shirt. He picked up a framed photo of the woman who lived there. "Come with daddy," he said, and pumped the photo on his crotch.

"Leave that alone," Bob said, and snatched the photo from his hand. "Out." Bob took Mann's arm and stood him up, but Mann shook him off.

"Don't touch me, bro." Mann adjusted his clothes as though Bob had rumpled them. Bob pointed Mann outside, locked the door behind them, then outpaced Mann as they headed for their trucks.

"You don't got a fucking right to touch me," Mann said. "You're the pissant in this company."

"Stop, you're hurting my feelings."

"Fuck you, Bob. You know, my old man he'd fire your ass if I told him to. I could've said how you doused that retard house."

Bob faced him. "You want to squeal, go ahead. I give a shit."

Mann grinned. His teeth glinted, razor sharp and pointed, in the sun. Bob stepped back, shut his eyes and swallowed. When he looked again, Mann's teeth were normal.

"Even though you are a dick," Mann said, "I got you something for passing."

Bob walked to his truck and peered in. A brown mutt lay in the bed, its head crushed and covered with green-backed flies.

"You killed this dog?" Bob asked.

"It's dead, ain't it?" Mann laughed so hard he held his belly.

"Get it out of my truck."

"You get it out. It's your present."

Bob stepped toward him, but Mann quickdrew his spray nozzle and squirted. The poison struck Bob in the eye, an ice pick driven into his pupil. He clawed at his contact lens.

"Ouch," Mann said.

Bob leaped at Mann, clutched his shirt and slung him to the concrete. Mann skidded, bellowing. Bob plucked the lens from his eye and blinked rapidly, tears streaming down his face, glanced at Mann on the ground, a pale blur. Bob sponged his eye with his handkerchief and spat into the lens. The pain quivered his knees.

"You're fired, asshole," Mann said.

Bob rubbed the lens with his thumb and put it back in. A fragment of hot steel. He bent over, then stood straight, lifted the dog from the truck and threw it hard into Mann, who scrambled away from the body.

Bob slid into his truck, cranked it and tore out. The ice pick drove deeper into his head, but he didn't stop. This was what it all came to. You tried to maintain a cool head and you ended up blinded and abused. You couldn't control even yourself because vicious bastards would always fuck you over.

Bob fishtailed around a corner and headed toward the interstate. He knew he would never be back with Tricia, would never get her out of him either. But he wouldn't let her be victim to some psycho. She hadn't been able to ask him to get rid of the fucker, so he'd do it on his own. He'd intercept Rick on the gravel road, block his way, threaten him, beat the shit out of him, use the knife if that's what it took. He'd show Tricia he'd been right. She'd see. Even if she didn't, at least part of his life would be settled again.

The fire surged across his forehead and into his other eye. Ahead, the interstate came into view, wavered, doubled. He pressed against the contact but the pain intensified. He careened onto the shoulder and screeched to a stop, plucked the tainted contact from his eye, put it in his mouth and squished saliva. Carefully he placed the circle onto his iris again, blinked and the burning was back, the tears flooding. He was damn near blind without it, but he popped the lens into his palm anyway. The burning began to subside almost immediately. He closed his fist on the lens, shut his good eye so that everything went blurry. He remembered himself and Tricia in the trailer, ashtrays overflowing with butts, empty cans on every surface, both of them exhausted, without energy to clean or fight. Quietly, politely, as if they were strangers, she had asked him to leave, and he had, knowing that he could right then before the anger returned.

He looked into the rearview mirror, his image indistinct, closed his bad eye and used only his good. His clear reflection surprised him, his dripping face screwed into a wink. He didn't look like a man going to hurt someone, he looked exhausted, like a man going home after work. Bob opened his fist. In his palm lay the soft contact. With his fingertips, he squashed the jelly oval, watched it pop up again, its shape and texture larval. He opened both eyes, making himself fuzzy, caught in an uncertain depth, then chuckled, braced and reinserted the contact. The pain rocketed through him, but he shifted into first and tore back into traffic.

# Roustabout

R. T. and I took a helicopter to work and we weren't rich men. We were roustabouts twenty-three miles offshore. A production platform, not a drilling rig, and I've got ten fingers to prove it. Out there, blue sky over us, blue sea under us, we pumped the vein, maybe even sucked from the heart. It thrilled me to think how deep we went.

Every other Thursday I drove south from Baton Rouge to Dulac—marsh grass, glare, and fish stench—and that's where I first saw him, R. T., melon shoulders, early balding head and sweet laugh, waiting for the chopper, drawing me like a big planet. Flying out, chuffing low over the last swamp before the gulf, he took me in, asking where from, when and why, none of that initiation ice the rest of the crew would give. Our quarters was a closet with two beds but that whole world was close, three stilted platforms connected at right angles by hovering catwalks, one three-story building perched eighty feet in the air, floors of honeycombed steel that fumbled bolts and wrenches fell through. At the platforms' highest levels a fall might kill you, at the lowest the gulf lapped the grating. Eight days on, six days off, seven men together more than half our lives.

R. T. and I listened to the same music—Sex Pistols, Ramones, Buzzcocks, The Damned—rare in 1979. Both of us planned on college. R. T. taught me the ropes and kept an eye on me. Second week out, standing under the crane arm, R. T. told me to move. Moments later, three fifty-five-gallon drums squashed the spot where I'd been. R. T. shook his head and pointed up. "Skarkey. Sloppy son of a bitch."

Evenings we ate, lifted weights, then took my guitar to the lower deck of the third platform. Water two feet below, we smoked a pin joint and sang as the sky purpled and oranged with sunset. R. T. told about his bride-to-be, Darlene, how fine and cool she was, then fretted over being with the same woman every day the rest of forever. I tried being sympathetic but I envied them their love and I shut him up by playing the Pistols' "Submission" as a ballad. During the chorus, fins sliced the surface, back and forth beneath the grating, sharks I thought, until two dolphins missiled from the drink and splashed us. From then on they came, Blow Holes 1 and 2, mates or pals we couldn't tell, barking like Flippers, sometimes letting us stroke their slick backs.

Next hitch, seven-foot swells bucking the boat we were on, R. T. and I lashed steel lines around a two-ton compressor and tried with our hands to steady its crane-rise off the deck. An errant swing bent a four-inch railing like straw and we danced not to be bent ourselves. When the compressor lifted above us, R. T. patted my shoulder and squeezed. That night I told R. T. about Bev, how we went to punk shows, cut each other's hair, went garage saleing, told him how the sex was good but not different, not hungry, not love. He flopped onto his side, propped his head on his hand and told me not to push and I'd find love, then said he had a crush on Nikki, the woman engineer who visited our platform once a week. He talked on, his voice as soft and even as warm surf. When he asked me a question, I didn't know where I was.

••

Slow work days we shared sights, thunderstorms stretching tendrils, bright fish schooling, ships passing in the distance. Once four waterspouts watusied side by side. Land was far away.

Sun-stupid one burning afternoon, I jerked on a valve cover and the cords in my back went with a squish. R. T. carried me to the tool shack, his chest against me, his arm around me. The company might cut me loose if they knew my back was bad, so R. T. and I sat, pain sweat shooting from me, R. T.'s hand kneading my neck. He told me work fuck-up stories but my ears were full of water rushing through a pipe and I covered my face and concentrated on his touch, firm and gentle, until my stomach swirled like a whirlpool. I clenched my body against his hand but I didn't tell him to take it away and before long he had to help me outside to puke. Walking, he pulled me up short and slipped his foot under a hinged section of floor grate we'd almost stepped through. He flipped it closed with a clang and my stomach lurched its contents through the floor and twenty-five feet down to the sump level where we'd almost gone. "Fucking Skarkey," R. T. said. "He left this hatch open before and didn't rope it." R. T. held me around the waist and I held him too as he ushered me inside again. "You okay?" he asked. The odor of diesel and grease hung strong and tears welled from my eyes but not from the smell and not from my back. From my heart. From the weirdness there.

••

Down by the water, R. T. talked his crush on Nikki and how he was lucky he could see she had a crush on me because that crush was saving him from something dumb that would foul his engagement. Nikki was the first woman any of the hands had seen on a platform and R. T. said it was all he could do not to linger on the fine, dark hairs at the base of her neck or on the way she bit her tongue whenever she read pressures. It was too much, R. T. speaking to me the problem I had with him, but the sharing of that feeling connected me to him in a way we hadn't had before. I banged out a punked-up chorus of "Torn Between Two Lovers" and we laughed and then R. T. said it bothered and scared him that he could be so close to marrying Darlene and still feel so drawn to Nikki. I said not to worry, his confusion came from being out here where you felt severed from the shore but I didn't buy the words myself. To feel better and pay back for the open hatch, we snuck into Skarkey's room and glued his boots to the floor.

Next morning at breakfast Skarkey sat next to Red, a number-one operator, and went on and on, cheerily, about how he knew Red had done the gluing because Skarkey's dad had probably done the same thing to Red in the old days. Red stewed, his face turning pinker and pinker, but he didn't say anything to Skarkey. Skarkey kept bugging Red, making R. T. and me nervous Red would turn on us, knowing we'd done it, until finally Red threw his breakfast in the trash and told us all to get our asses in gear.

We were wary because the least thing could send Red nuclear, flinging pipe wrenches and cursing and once in a while hurting himself. His list of injuries was epic: butt cheek impaled on a needle-nose valve, pinkie lopped off by the safety-capsule's hatch, kneecap cracked stumbling from a chopper. His nickname came from his bright pink skin caused years ago when a toilet he'd been on blew up. Story was, somebody hooked a gas line to a newfangled electric commode that was supposed to burn crap instead of flush it (you tell me how) and when Red finished his business and dropped a cigarette between his legs, the crapper blew him through a door. The company promised him a foreman's job if he didn't sue. Fifteen years later promotion still wasn't in sight.

The rest of the day Red had us cleaning sand and sludge out of the separator tank, popping by to tell us how piss poor we were doing. He put Skarkey in charge of us and Skarkey rode us, "Do it right, goddamnit, do it over," while he lummoxed to the side until late in the afternoon R. T. said Skarkey needed to quit doing us up the butt. I flinched but Skarkey threw a wrench down on the grating and called R. T. a cocksucker, one of Red's favorite expressions. R. T. faced Skarkey and ha-ha'ed and Skarkey breathed hard, his oversized hands flailing and boat feet stamping until he spat and trudged off.

"Freak," R. T. said. "We best keep an eye out."

••

Next day Nikki arrived and R. T.'s crush got the best of him, his eyes going moist when she wielded a crescent or stretched to view a high gauge, his eyes going the way I knew my eyes sometimes went when I watched him. Red saw this happening and mouthed off how the only thing better than fucking a woman engineer would be fucking a dolphin hole. Me and R. T. laughed despite ourselves and Red even joined in.

Nikki asked me to hop with her to a satellite platform to collect a pig we'd run through a line and R. T.'s shoulders went droopy even though he managed a wink for me. The pilot, a Nam vet, skimmed the chopper five feet from the water to test our cool, then dropped us on the platform while he made some more runs. It only took me a couple of minutes to retrieve the pig, a large plug of plastic that rootered paraffin out of lines, and then Nikki suggested we sit in the shade and wait. A nice breeze blew and she took off her hard hat and boots and socks and rubbed her ankles and wiggled her toes.

"Look," she said and pointed. In the shadow of the

platform, five barracudas hung motionless in a V. "I'll bet they'd like it if we went skinny-dipping." She laid back, her hat a pillow, and I laid back too and watched a wispy cloud pass over us.

"Nimbus," I said.

"And you haven't even been to college yet," she said.

Natural gas hissed through pipes and I was drifting off when Nikki said she wished it could be peaceful out here all the time. She talked about growing up in New Jersey and going to the beach and how much colder and grayer Atlantic water was than gulf. Said she'd never been to Baton Rouge and asked if I wouldn't show her around some time if she came over from Lafayette. We were quiet again and then she poked me in the arm and said, "Hey, Ray, want to hear about geologic time?," smiling her slightly buck-toothed smile, strands of black hair arcing across her forehead. She took me back in history to the cooling of magma and then up to the dinosaurs and the giant primordial rain forests, brought me on through the dinosaurs' fall and the rotting of the forests and their burial under layers of sediment all the way to their transformation into oil and retrieval by drilling. Nobody had ever talked to me like that, talked me through time and change and then taken me with them down into the earth on the head of a diamond drill bit and I noticed a silver glint in the deep almond of her eyes. I asked her to join me and R. T. after supper but she said she had to leave early the next day and couldn't and we sat quietly then dozed until the chopper's blades batting the air woke us.

That night R. T. pined for Nikki and I tried not to look too much at him, both of us singing seventies love ballads that seemed to make Blow Holes 1 and 2 crash excessively into the water, wetting us all over. Then while we were asleep, a moored supply boat bumped against a platform leg, sending tremors through us. I awakened thinking we were going down but R. T.'s snores filling the tiny cabin settled me. I eased out of bed and stood next to him, studying the calm of his sleeping face, smelling the salty smell he put off. R. T. bolted awake, "What is it?!" and my limbs went chilly and I blurted he'd been having a nightmare and I was waking him up. He pushed against his eyes then pulled back the covers to reveal a bulge in his underwear.

"Not a nightmare," he said, grinning, "Nikki."

••

Sticky dawn to steamy dusk I watched a ship tow a platform across the horizon, moving more slowly than the sun. I wished I could be there when they toppled it from the barge—the splash, the sink, the settle. Onshore, Bev and I hung, buying records, taking speed, going dancing at the Damn Shame. After a Shitdogs' show, Bev made me shave half her head, then I had her cut mine short but not too strange. Still, Dennis our foreman called me punk rocker. Bev and I slept together sometimes but it was no big love thing and we knew it.

Nevertheless, I'd wake up, Bev asleep next to me, her white lipstick and eye makeup glowing in the dark, and feel middle-distanced and distracted and dishonest yet relieved to find I was still turned on.

Next shift these rough-looking riggers flew to our platform with a super-eight projector and some porno flicks to show in the rec room. R. T. and I laughed at one called *Barnyard Fun* featuring fucking with pigs, chickens, dogs, and a stallion. The riggers took to hooting and slapping each other a lot and Red said he was leaving before somebody tried to hump him. Skarkey followed, raising R. T.'s eyebrows. During the next movie, the riggers started eyeing us and talking about young meat so much we snuck out and hid in the third-platform tool shack, absolutely black and still with the odor of crude. I sensed R. T. more than I could see him and I wanted to tell him, just blurt it out, but I pictured R. T. reacting, not mean or violent, simply roping off our conversations, amending the affection we already had. I picked up a bolt and started screwing the nut up and down as I heard the harsh laughter of the riggers travel from the first platform across the quiet water. In a sad voice R. T. said that how we felt right then must be how Nikki always felt.

••

A few days later Nikki joined us for our sing. She marvelled at how nice it was by the twilight water and said that this was the first time she'd ever fully relaxed out here. R. T. told some funny Red injury stories but I drifted and had a vision of the three of us swimming in the twilight, R. T.'s wide shoulders slick with salt water, Nikki's black hair pasted back from the dark brown of her face. Blow Holes 1 and 2 brought me out of it, rocketing from the water and breaking Nikki into a laugh with gusto we'd never heard from her before. Dripping, Nikki leaned down and stroked Blow Hole 1 on the nose, making him chatter madly, while R. T. pulled his knees to his chest and stared at the scene like some lovesick kid, just like I knew I was doing to him. He excused himself and left.

When he was gone Nikki said she hated when the platform oil-slicked the sea and thought new engineers like her, maybe even like me someday, could clean up some of the old ways. Then she talked how it pissed her off that hands who knew half what she did about the platform treated her without respect, but it made her the maddest that Red would always keep her an outsider and never try to share what he knew. The way her brown eyes fired when she talked made me see fully what R. T. had been seeing.

Back at the main platform, Nikki and I found the kitchen hands, stoned and laughing, throwing scraps to sharks thrashing the water below. It was a wild contrast to the calmness of the third platform and I swallowed thinking about my feet dangling in that water only a few minutes ago. Red happened by and yelled at the hands did they know what would happen if the platform went down some night at suppertime and there would be all these sharks trained to feed? He was right, of course, and we all went solemn and Red looked at Nikki and asked did they teach all the sense out of her at college. When he was gone, Nikki asked me whether Red had to practice to be such an asshole or did it come natural.

••

On land, I told Bev I couldn't stay over and she asked me why our good fun thing was fizzling. I told her the truth. She paced back and forth and cried and called me a fag. Then she apologized and told me she understood because she had once been in love with her best friend, a woman, for two years and had never told her and finally her best friend had gone off with another woman. Bev changed clothes into black tights and a ripped Clash T-shirt and cried some more and said she'd been confused about where we were going since we never had really loved each other that way and she got mad all over again and changed clothes again and said I'd used her and how long had I been sleeping with her while I was in love with a man. She said she'd miss my skin in bed with her and the way I cut her hair and maybe we could still sleep together and play makeup and pogo and then she told me to get the hell out and called me when I got home to tell me all the same things again and we ended up crying together.

I spent the rest of my days off wondering if I should just tell R. T. to get it off my chest, no matter if it would change our friendship or not, but I knew that if I told him he could never feel the same about me again. I was scared too of the hands doing something to hurt me or at least never being comfortable around me again or Dennis firing me just because I loved people regardless of their genitals. Then, oddly, I started thinking where I'd take Nikki if she ever came to Red Stick to see me. By the time I went back out, I felt like a well pumped dry.

••

After supper R. T. and I lifted weights like we often did except neither of us said much until as I was lifting the barbell from his chest he said, "What's wrong with me, man?" I gave a start because I'd been staring at his pecs and bobbled the weights before I settled them into the bench support. He exhaled through his nose and laid there gazing at the ceiling. "At home I'm crazy about Darlene but as soon as I get out here I start thinking about that Yankee engineer. Maybe I'm schizo."

"It's just cold feet," I said.

"Maybe," he said and swung his legs around and sponged the towel on his slick head. "It's so sexy the way Nikki knows so much about the process. She doesn't take any shit either. I can talk to her a way I could never talk to Darlene."

My eyes were bugging with pressure and I blurted, "I broke up with Bev."

R. T. stood and put a hand on my shoulder. "I'm sorry, dude," he said. "I didn't know."

I moved away from his hand and put my back to the wall. "No big deal," I said. "We're still friends."

"It is a big deal. I know y'all were tight. Buddies. Shit, buddies are as important as lovers, maybe more important."

"Let me do my reps," I said and came over and sat on the bench.

R. T. looked at nothing, his fingers on his chin, until suddenly he pointed at me. "You know what," he said, "you oughta ask Nikki out."

"Nikki?"

"Yeah. You know she digs you."

"I don't know. What about you and the way you, you know . . ."

"Fuck her and me. This would be perfect." He walked across the room rubbing his palms and nodding. "I can't go for her and if you were seeing her that might straighten my head out. Plus, you're free now. I mean, if you want to see her."

I saw Nikki's angular face, her intense gaze. "I like her. She told me about dinosaur times."

"There you go."

I laid back on the bench, warm and moist from R. T.'s sweat. He leaned over and looked into my eyes so deep I reached up and tried to lift the bar myself. R. T. held it down and shook his head.

"Why can't it be simple," he asked, "like it is between us?"

••

Next day, our foreman, Dennis, who'd been on platforms for years but seemed to be expert only at playing bourrée, stepped with both boots into Red's cool about a problem Red had nothing to do with but Skarkey did. We'd been having compressor problems and then late the night before a couple of serious pump problems and then right before sunup a leak had hissed a cloud of natural gas into the still air putting everybody on edge. Red kept trying to talk but Dennis interrupted him every time saying he was sick of excuses and all he wanted to hear from Red was that the job had been done right. Red, I swear, turned tomato and had to jam his fists in his pockets where I could see them working like little animals. The weird thing that happened though was Skarkey inching in close until he was about a foot from Dennis and shifting his glare between Dennis and Red like he was watching a tennis match. Skarkey loomed over Dennis and looked sinister behind the black-rimmed, tinted safety glasses he always wore and after Red stalked off and we all started to drift away Skarkey glared so hard at Dennis that Dennis had to ask if he had a problem. Skarkey leaned down and said, "Red's the best. The best." Skarkey's dad evidently still had powerful allies in the company because Dennis just told Skarkey to take a roustabout and do a safety check, then closed himself inside his office.

R. T. had asked me if he could work with Nikki that day so he could look his crush thing in the eye and I'd agreed, so I volunteered to go with Skarkey. I had to pace to keep up with his angry strides and he kept muttering, "Dennis got no right, he got no right," and so on until I swear I wanted to hug him for loving Red so much and not being ashamed of it. I ended up taking the caps off all the fire extinguishers, three-foot-tall canisters, and stirring the powder and making sure the hoses were clear while Skarkey stood peering across to the next platform where Red, R. T., and Nikki were working. I had just opened the final extinguisher on that platform when Skarkey turned to me and said, "I know your secret." I bobbled the extinguisher and dropped it belching a big puff of white powder out of the open top and into my face. I choked and coughed and when I finally managed to clear my eyes, Skarkey had the same expression as before and was standing in the same spot as if we'd glued his boots right there.

My legs jellied and I didn't know what to say so I brushed my hands together. Still I figured if Skarkey had found out either no one would believe him or everybody knew or it would take the weight off me or maybe R. T. might react positively or I'd just quit and take my bruises to land with me.

"What secret?" I asked, wondering how powdery my face was.

"How you like that girl engineer," Skarkey blurted and broke into a laugh that bent him double and made him slap his knee. I'd never heard anybody laugh like that, almost orgasmic, his face going all cartoonish, and by the time he focused on me I felt my own mouth stretched into some sort of acid grin. Skarkey shoved me so hard I stumbled backward, his attempt at comradeship, and then I started laughing a laugh as freakish as his, my frustration and confusion spewing from me thick and clotted, until I noticed his expression had gone serious and he was peering off toward Red and the others again.

"I like her, too," he said. "She ain't mean."

I never expected to feel kinship with Skarkey the way I did right then but immediately he told me to hurry so we could check the life raft and move to the platform the others were on, which irritated me since I would have already been finished if he'd been helping. To see was there dry rot in the canvas-mesh bottom of the raft, we hoisted the 200-pound rectangle of hard plastic onto our shoulders. One of the oar hooks snagged my shirt and just as I was about to tell Skarkey to hold on so I could unhook, Red called for Skarkey over the P.A. Skarkey dropped his end and the hook in my heavy cotton sleeve dragged me down to the grating. Pinned, I called after Skarkey but he hustled off oblivious, leaving me to rip my shirt to get loose. Sleeve torn I went after him, my knee bleeding, my shoulder bruised, and worse, my back throbbing.

I found him on the second platform with Red, Nikki, and R. T. where Red was in Skarkey's face about connecting a wrong line that could've killed the three of them. Red's eyes bulged like olives and he poked his finger into Skarkey's chest, every poke hitting Skarkey like a punch. I'd never seen Red go off on Skarkey like this and R. T., Nikki, and I glanced at each other as Skarkey said shaky-voiced over and over, "No problem, no problem," the exact perfect phrase to blow a gasket in Red. Red charged on into Skarkey, calling him a dickless misfit his father should've jacked off on the wall and Skarkey's hands started to gesture and quiver in between him and Red. Red saw them and took a half-step backwards. He sneered at Skarkey's hands and told him, "Stop doing that, goddamnit, be a man." Skarkey held his hands to his chest for a moment, then sort of staggered forward, reaching out and grabbing Red's shirt in what was a plea but came off clumsy and rough. In a flash, Red slapped Skarkey's face, slapped it hard, and shoved him. "Get off me, you fucking queer," Red spat and brushed his shirt where Skarkey had touched him before storming away toward the third platform.

Skarkey took off his hard hat and blubbered, outright blubbered, as he stared after Red's back shrinking down the catwalk. When he noticed us watching him, he shoved me and screamed, "Stupid fuck," then strode after Red, the perfect response for somebody who'd just had the person he admires the most testify he was an outsider, a goofball, a misfit.

We finished the job in a few minutes, none of us saying much, and headed to the third platform to finish the maintenance check me and Skarkey had started. We heard some yelling and then Skarkey came straight at us on the catwalk, his face blotched, a bright streak of blood trailing from his nose, and brushed past us like we were see-through. "Looks like they had a conference," R. T. said and we kept on, hoping Red wouldn't think we were tracking him. Just as we reached the third platform Red cut around the corner of the tool shed, eyes levelled, and disappeared through the floor. We watched him fall and nobody made a sound until Red hit the sump-level with a clanging thud. A hideous moan billowed up and I was running to catch Nikki and R. T. who were blazing toward where we sat evenings.

The clunking steps down seemed a hundred miles long and at the bottom Red's legs were bent all wrong and his faded blue eyes stared up at the gap in the grating. Nikki knelt talking to him, telling him to be still, and R. T. told me run get help and then I was moving and hearing the clomp of my own boots on metal even though it seemed like my legs weren't my legs at all.

••

That evening the three of us went down to the water and R. T. stared toward shore, scraping at grease under his fingernails and once in a while forcing a laugh at something I played. None of us really looked where Red had crashed or talked about Red's injuries or Skarkey's intent or arrest. Nikki took off her shoes and rolled her pants up to her knees and let the gentle swells reach and touch her feet and shins. The scene was fouled with sadness and I wanted to touch my palm to R. T.'s face just as I'm sure he wanted to touch his to Nikki's, two things that wouldn't be.

I was picking out "Psychotherapy" when R. T. stood and climbed the stairs without a word. Nikki and I watched him trudge across the catwalks, a small figure suspended high above the water just before dark. Sadness was chewing at me and then Nikki said, "Christ, I love it out here." She lifted her feet out of the water and turned toward me and extended her legs, her feet brown and high-arched.

"R. T.'s got it bad for you," I said.

"I know," she said. "He's engaged. And he's too macho." She stretched, pressing her shirt tight against her small breasts, then rubbed her chin. "He does look at the gulf like you and I do, though. He knows how marvelous it is." The last of the sunset played off her eyes and she smiled and Blow Holes 1 and 2 popped up right on cue. Nikki laid on her stomach and petted them and they talked to her and she to them and I serenaded them all until Nikki came over and sat beside me.

"You think Red'll be all right?" I asked.

"He wasn't all right before," she said.

"True."

"I doubt he'll walk right, but at least he's not paralyzed."

"Maybe he'll finally sue the company."

She smoothed her hand across the belly of my guitar, laying next to me, and said, "What do you think'll happen to Skarkey?"

I shrugged. "It won't be happy whatever it is."

Nikki pulled her knees up close to her chest and wiggled her small toes. "It must be hard to be like Red and not love anything. I can tell he used to love this place. Now he doesn't belong."

The Blow Holes chattered and Nikki held her hands out in the air too far away to touch them. "You think they love each other?" I asked and she held her palms up. The water had gone dark below the last orange belt on the horizon and Nikki stood and unbuttoned her shirt, unzipped her jeans and stepped free. Her skin was dark except for pale stripes across her breasts and hips and her abdomen swelled out like a tiny dolphin's head. I glanced back toward the first platform and she dove and sliced into the water. Blow Holes 1 and 2 screamed with delight and circled Nikki and she let her palms run across their backs, their bodies big and sleek.

"Is it safe?" I asked.

"The sharks won't bother me with the dolphins here," she said.

Nikki stroked the dolphins and swam with them until one of the Blow Holes nudged her hard then nudged her again and kind of pushed her down and the other Blow Hole bumped against him or her and chattered. My heart ballooned a little toward my throat and the aggressive Blow Hole dunked Nikki again. I shot up ready to go in, the dolphins huge next to Nikki, and wished R. T. were there but then Nikki surfaced close to the platform and reached for the grating as the Blow Holes butted each other ten feet away.

I bent and grasped her wrists, her hair plastered from her bright face, the Blow Holes cackling, and tugged her.

Pain fired from my back through my brain but I lifted her and then clutched myself, water springing from my eyes. Nikki touched me, her wet body close and boyish except for the long curves of her waist and the wonderful round of her behind which were coming through to me despite the sear along my spine. Then everything blended and I dropped to my butt.

"How bad is it?" she asked.

"Locked," I said.

Through the hurt I watched her dress and tried not to think that only hours before Red had lain where I was laying. The Blow Holes sailed and flopped sending their splashes onto us and Nikki knelt and wrapped her arms around me from behind. She lifted and I grunted, the damp circles of her breasts pressing against me, the loop of her hug strong across my chest.

"Can you walk?" she asked.

"I think," I said.

I draped an arm over her wiry shoulders and she held my waist as we started up the steps. My back muscles were taut burning ropes but Nikki supported me on the climb and on our slow way across the catwalks, blue cones of light spilling over the metal and down to the water.

"I can't let Dennis see me," I said.

"He's playing cards. We'll get you to your room."

Electric shocks traced my hamstrings with each step and Nikki squeezed me and I squeezed my eyes against my swimmy head and when we finally reached the stairs to my quarters I told her I didn't think I could make it.

"Let's go to mine," she said and we eased beneath the window of the rec room where laughter crackled over us then limped around to the rear where Nikki's was. She unlocked her door and I thought how sad it was that she needed a key when none of us did and then I thought of Red's twisted legs and Skarkey's bloody nose and even Bev's puffy eyes and my chest quavered as Nikki led me to her bed. She gentled me onto my stomach and when I hit the mattress I broke into hot-faced heaving. I tried to stem it but when Nikki laid her hands on the cramping cords paralleling my backbone I melted into sobs no shame could stop.

••

My eyelids cracked open and I felt the sway of the platform beneath me and a body beside me. I thought of R. T. through a haze of exhaustion until I turned my head and met the deep brown of Nikki's look as she woke up. "Hi," she said and smiled.

"How long I been out?" I asked.

She glanced at her watch and said, "Several hours. I massaged your back and it loosened a little, then you zonked. You were mumbling a lot for a while."

"Sorry. Sorry about the crying, too."

"It's been a hell of a day," she said.

"A shitty day," I said.

I torqued myself onto my side and slid my legs off the bed and creaked to my feet. My muscles felt rusty and gunked but the fire and tension had definitely diminished. Nikki got up and came over.

"You don't have to go yet," she said and it took me a minute to see what she meant. I considered it, her body against mine, her lips on my lips, the two of us spooned against the violence of the day.

"I need to get back. It'd look weird."

"Can you make it upstairs?"

"Yeah. Your massage helped. You helped."

Nikki stepped close and hugged me and I hugged her too and then she kissed and I kissed back for a moment until I had to pull away.

"Was that bad?" she asked.

"No, that was good. It's just I'm getting over somebody."

I stepped to the door and opened it, glanced at her sharp features in the dim light. "Thanks, Nikki."

"See you tomorrow, Ray."

I closed the door behind me and waded into the moist air. The wind had kicked up phosphorous whitecaps and vibrations through the steel, and the platform hissed and groaned. Salt stickied my skin and I remembered the day we tested the emergency slide, me and R. T., the slide popping yellow and wide and unrolling from high up down to the water. We skimmed its cushion and splashed in the warm drink, salt like sex smell, splashed and dunked each other and looked up to the operators, Red number one and Skarkey number two, laughing against the sky.

Twinges shot through my legs and I flinched but I held the handrail and climbed the stairs, the image of

Skarkey in handcuffs and weeping for Red igniting in my mind like a burn-off flare. At the top I leaned on the wall and breathed before I crept down the hall to our quarters.

R. T. flicked on the light when I came in and once he focused he grinned a big grin and said, "You dog, you goddamn dog." I sat on the chair, hiding the ache, and smiled back at him. He swung out of bed and leaned close over me and breathed in then let out an "Ahhh." I wanted more than ever to tell him the truth, the truth about everything, but in my head Red's shocky eyes gazed at nothing. I shivered.

"How was it?" he asked.

"Great," I said. "Really great."

He patted me on the shoulder and sat on his bed then looked at the floor, his big scuffed mitts splayed on his hairy knees.

"That's good," he said and nodded. "That's real good."

Through my soles and calves and knees came trembles rising from the metal legs plunged into currents deep and uncertain. I straightened my back.

"R. T.," I said and he met my eyes again. "I hope you don't mind, but I thought of you."

# The Smell of a Car

There's nothing like the smell of a clean car, that crisp
aroma of vinyl upholstery and spotless plastic. It gives you
a good feeling, a feeling like I used to get after Evelyn
and I straightened the house, a feeling like everything's
set in order. And that's the feeling I was enjoying that
morning as I sat in the parking lot where I'm warehouse
foreman, sipping a Coke and planning the orders we had
to get out that day. The warm spring air drifted through
my window, free of the caustic bauxite odor we usually
got from the aluminum plant. Across Choctaw Street
three black kids tightroped a railroad track, their arms
held out for balance. They kept slipping off, laughing
and shoving each other and I was smiling at them even
though, for some reason, they reminded me that Evelyn
was gone.

Just then these two pickups slid in, one behind the
other, throwing shells as their wheels ground to a stop.
The man in the second pickup, a tall bony guy (Triche
was his name I later learned), jumped out carrying a
shot-gun. He hesitated a moment behind the first
truck's cab, gave a quick look inside, then stuck the
gun barrel through the window and fired. The shot
sounded muffled, not nearly as loud as the shot man's

scream, which cut straight to my spine. Triche stepped back, crouching and stretching his neck to see what he'd done. He ejected the empty cartridge and stared at the shotgun as if he'd just realized it was there. Then, as if a line connected us, his eyes rose to me, still behind the wheel.

Triche started toward me, walking very slow, the gun across his body, his boots on the shells like somebody chewing bone. The taste of bacon and eggs came up in my mouth and even though my car wasn't running, I had the accelerator floored. I wished for a second I had the pistol I carried when I worked late doing inventory books, but by then Triche had stopped a few feet from my car. His finger was still on the trigger.

"That'll show him," he said, his pupils screwed tight inside his bright green eyes. He was about my age, early thirties. He wore a flowered baseball cap turned backwards, an "Eat Oysters, Love Longer" T-shirt, and loose, faded jeans—boilermaker clothes—and the thought that he'd probably worked with pipe we sold popped into my head. He lowered his head like he was trying to work spit into his mouth. A string of curses came from the wounded man still in his truck, and Triche gritted his teeth and wrinkled his nose like he felt the pain.

"He rammed me and took off over on Mission," he said. A shiver jolted him. Then he walked back to his own truck, a new Ford with a crumpled quarter panel, turned off his engine, and replaced the gun on the rack.

I felt wetness in my pants, then saw the Coke can crushed in my hands and some of the drink spilled on my lap. The letters on our building—Louisiana Pipe Supply—were pulsing. The kids on the track had run away, but several other black people had come out in their backyards and were peering across Choctaw to see what was going on. Alan, my boss, and some of the guys who work under me in the warehouse pulled the wounded man from the truck and laid him out on the white shells. His lower stomach was mixed with his shirt and pants, and Alan pressed a towel against the wound, making the man draw in his breath.

I opened the car door and stepped out, but the slack string in my legs made me hang onto the door for a second before heading over. The hurt man was older, in his sixties, a thick, big-necked man with gray hair and a face that might have been ruddy but was pale and loose now. The towel soaked reddish brown as the man moved his head from side to side, I guess trying to shake what had happened to him out of his mind. His name was Strickland, but I didn't know that yet.

Someone touched my shoulder and I jerked around to Triche standing beside me. He leaned back for a moment, then said, "He went for a piece," low, as if he was sharing a secret. "You seen it." A large drop of sweat coursed down his face.

"I don't know what I saw," I said.

Triche looked at Strickland and squeezed his own cheeks with his hand. "Shit," he said in a whisper.

"You bastard, you shot me," Strickland said, and pointed. He laid his head back and pressed his hands to his sides.

"He liked to killed me running into my truck," Triche said to all of us, but he finished by looking at me. "You seen him go for his glove box. You know what happened. You know me."

And I saw that I did know him, remembered that I'd talked to him about fishing once when he came into the warehouse to buy some PVC pipe for his bathroom.

"You better go to your truck," I said.

Triche grunted as if I'd poked him. "Make sure you tell 'em what you saw," he said, then he walked back, sat down on his bumper and rubbed a finger back and forth across his teeth.

"Oh, I'm sick," Strickland said, and his milky blue eyes, glistening with fear, locked on me, I guess because I was standing near his feet. He breathed much more quickly, and I felt my own blood draining out of me, had a selfish thought that I hoped he waited to die because I didn't want to see it. I heard sirens in the distance, and Strickland raised his knees and began moving his feet back and forth, clearing two ruts with his white tennis shoes. Alan told him to try and be still.

It seems strange, but I crouched and put a hand on his knee. "The ambulance is almost here," I said, and he nodded.

"Call my daughter," he said straight at me. "Caitlin Strickland. In Dallas."

"We'll tell the police," Alan said.

Strickland was already in the ambulance before the police got there. They handcuffed Triche, and he jerked his head at me while he was telling them what had happened. As Triche passed me in the police car, he nodded as if to say, You understand what I did.

"Miller, you know that crazy asshole?" Alan asked.

"I met him once," I said. David, the new guy in the warehouse, started washing the shells with a hose. Alan followed me over to Strickland's truck, which the police had moved out of the way along with Triche's. The seat was a mess. I tried the handle, but of course it was locked. "Christ, I can't believe the cops left it that way," I said. "They didn't leave a key?"

"They said it's the family's responsibility."

The water David sprayed splashed on the shells, combining the blood with mud underneath. I stared until the spot seemed only a couple of inches from my eyes. "Seems too soon to wash it away," I said.

••

My kitchen was dark except for a tangled pattern of orange on the wall, the day's last sunlight thrown through the plants on the windowsill. I took a beer from the fridge and drank half of it before I went into the living room and sat in my chair. I wanted to savor the fact that we'd finished all of the day's work and had started on the next day, but a sensation like I used to have when I took cheap speed to work nights was creeping up on me. The clock on the other side of the room seemed far away, like fever was distorting my depth perception. I listened to its ticking, listened closely, waiting for the feeling it was stirring in me to become a memory like I knew it would. In the parking lot, after everyone had gone, the two trucks cooling. Tick, tick, tick. Such an unlikely connection. I remembered Strickland's cry when he was shot, more a sound of disbelief and fear than pain. My own body odor surrounded me.

I stood. Evelyn had been gone eight months, but the house had never been emptier than this night. For the first time in weeks, I wanted to call her, but I knew how distant she would be. As distant as she'd accused me of being. Passive-aggressive she called me. She said somewhere along the way I'd stepped out of the marriage and into being critical, uninvolved, passionless, dead. Words more and more designed to goad me into fighting the way she wanted me to, with screams and crashing. I had never let her.

I started out the door, then returned to our bedroom and reached down the holstered .38 I took with me when I stayed late at work by myself. Before I got in my car, I righted the lean in the For Sale sign in the front yard, then looked up and down the street. I noticed how many bass boats, three-wheelers, and raised four-wheel-drive pickups sat in the yards and under the carports of the brick ranch houses on our street. Evelyn and I had stretched our budget to move here from North Baton Rouge, trying to get away from the older part of town where break-ins were a constant fear and what was going on in the houses around us seemed so close it bled over. But that night, my pistol in my hand, I imagined my neighbors' guns. On their walls. In their vehicles. More guns maybe than people.

••

At the hospital downtown, I bypassed the elevator and pushed through a heavy door into the stairwell. I was halfway up the stairs when the door clanged shut behind me. I spun and crouched, little shocks spitting through me, then held the bannister and breathed deep, embarrassed even though nobody was there.

By the time I reached the fourth floor, I was steady again. I rubbed my hands against the cold of the long hall that led to intensive care, wondering if Strickland was still alive. Above the door a red-light sign said "No Visitors." In the waiting room, a few people huddled in groups, but none of them seemed shocked enough to be Strickland's people. I wandered until I saw the smoking section, a small room set off to the side. Through the window in the door, I saw a woman in a gray dress and jacket, a professional's clothes. She sat bent at the waist and stared at the wall. Her eyes were the color of Strickland's. A pink rash covered her throat. When I entered, she straightened, a big-boned woman with a wide square face and wavy black hair to her shoulders. She wasn't smoking, but the smoke in the room was thick nevertheless. I figured she'd come in here to get away.

"Are you with Mr. Strickland?" I asked.

"Who are you?" she said, standing, her eyes wide, her

hands linked in front of her breasts. Maybe my work clothes had made her think I was the man who'd shot her father.

"I'm Miller Terrell. I was there, at work, this morning when he got shot."

"Do you know him?"

"I just wanted to find out how he was."

"He's dying," she said, her voice controlled but tight like it had too much pressure on it. "The doctor says it's only a matter of time." She looked a little older than I was, but it was hard to tell because she looked so tired. "Would you like to sit down?"

"Maybe we could walk down and get some coffee," I said, wanting to get to some fresher air. "I could use some."

She nodded, and I picked up the shoulder-strapped night bag she had. The air in the hall was cool and fresh, but my temples had started throbbing. We didn't talk in the elevator, the whir of the cables filling the space and making me imagine thin strands lowering us in the shaft. When we reached the cafeteria, she went to the far corner and lit a cigarette while I got us some coffee.

She formally introduced herself when I sat. Her handshake was firm and hard. "I flew in from Dallas as soon as I heard. Dad was already in a coma when I arrived." She took a deep drag. "Did you see what happened?"

"I saw the shooting. I didn't see what caused it. It happened about eight this morning."

"Quite a start to the day, huh?" she said and smiled,

but then she took a Kleenex out of her purse and wiped her nose. "It seems like a week since the call came. I was at work." She blew on her coffee, then watched me as she sipped. "I haven't cried at all. I almost cried when the police gave me the news, but afterwards I just felt numb."

"You're probably in shock."

"I don't think so. I believe it's seeing him with those tubes and machines. They make him seem unreal."

"You have any relatives around here?"

"No. My mother died three years ago and I'm an only child. I was living in Chicago until last year. I saw Dad a few months ago." She flicked her cigarette into the ashtray. Her hand was shaking. "Dad's somewhat of a loner. Most of their friends were Mother's, so when she died it left him pretty isolated. In fact, he and I have only really been in contact with each other since I moved south again. I've been thinking about all that lost time." Her cigarette hand shook worse, and she covered it with her other. "I'm sorry," she said. "I barely know you."

"That's all right," I said.

"I've only talked to doctors today. I've been around all these other families and friends of families, and I don't have the slightest idea who Dad might want me to call. That's a shame, isn't it, to be so cut off?"

A clatter exploded from the kitchen, and I jerked, spilling my coffee. I bolted up before it ran into my lap, and my vision went bright white, ringing like feedback swelling in my ears. Blind, I reached for the table, put my hands in warm coffee and pulled them back. Caitlin's voice came through asking me if I was okay, and by then the ringing was falling, my sight coming back.

"Stood up too fast," I said. She was standing, too. "What a mess."

"Maybe you should go home," she said.

The panic I'd felt at home swept through me again. I shivered.

"I already went home."

I took napkins from the dispenser and wiped the coffee from my hands. Caitlin spread napkins on top of the spill, brown stains spreading and soaking the white squares in a second. She gathered the sopping papers, dark liquid dripping through her fingers, and stuffed them in my cup.

"Your father told me to call you," I said.

Caitlin sponged her hands and looked directly into my eyes, her eyes bringing back her father's. She crumpled the napkin and tossed it onto the table. "They'll let two people in if we don't stay long," she said.

In the elevator she stared at the numbered buttons. The splotch on her neck had shrunk some.

"Do you know the man who shot Dad?"

"I've done some business with him."

"What is he like?"

I wanted to call him crazy or vicious, but the image that came to mind was Triche in the warehouse showing me a homemade fishing fly he kept on his key ring, an image I didn't know I had. "Mean, I guess," I said.

The oxygen-fat air in Strickland's cubicle cleared my head, but I wished it hadn't since it just made me more aware of the respirator heaving and sucking like a hydraulic pump. Caitlin held his wrist and stared at the heart monitor, not talking to him. I didn't agree that Strickland seemed less real, just less alive, his skin pasty, his eyes slitted and cloudy. After a couple of minutes, Caitlin said, "I'll meet you outside," and left.

Maybe it was morbid to stay, but I don't think it was. Since that morning it was the most connected I'd felt, strangely, the most connected I'd felt in a while. I walked to Strickland's side. "Mr. Strickland, you don't know me," I said. "I was there when you got hurt." I searched for something else to say, but all I could think was how I wished I could stay in that room until he died, how it seemed like this room was the only place I should be until he was gone. I glanced through the glass to make sure no one was looking, then I picked up Mr. Strickland's hand in both of mine. His hand was warm and fleshy and oddly calming, even though it was completely strange to be holding someone's hand. I squeezed it, and his eyes twitched in a way I like to think wasn't some reflex. "I won't forget you," I said, and it didn't, it still doesn't, seem ridiculous.

••

In the waiting room again, I asked Caitlin if there was anything I could do.

"Take me to get Dad's truck," she said.

"I can get somebody to do that."

She took a knot of keys from her purse and let them lie on her palm. "Take me."

"The truck's a mess, Caitlin. It's been closed up all day."

She balled her fist around the keys. "I want to go," she said, but I looked away. "Miller, can you say why you came here?" I didn't look at her. "You can't, can you? You should understand then."

The spot on my car seat was sticky even though I'd cleaned the Coke on it. Caitlin's smell—cigarette smoke and a sweet dry aroma like hand lotion—filled the humid air in my car. No one had been in that seat since Evelyn and for a moment a feeling of elation, like a first date, flashed over me, then a heaviness at knowing Evelyn was never going to sit in that seat again, a thought I hadn't had before.

The quickest route was down 38th, a way I'd taken hundreds of times, but that night the closed-up stores and run-down houses crowded the road. A drizzle had slicked the streets while I was in the hospital, and stoplights streaked the road red in front of us. The far-off refinery stacks spat flames into the low clouds.

"It's like the whole city's on fire," Caitlin said.

"They burn more on overcast nights. E.P.A. regulations. I guess you get used to it," I said, but then I couldn't stop watching the fire curl into the sky's belly. The car rumbled over railroad tracks, and I turned onto Choctaw, the same path Triche and Strickland had taken. My tires crunched on the shells, and I stopped at the spot where Triche's truck had stopped. Caitlin stared past me at the two pickups parked off to the side. She lit a cigarette, and I didn't say anything or crack a window even though the smoke burned my nose. I ran my eyes over the building's windows, making sure the right lights were burning, then touched my pistol beneath the seat.

"Where exactly did it happen?" she asked, her face shadowed.

"Right up there. The men from the warehouse laid him on the shells."

She stepped out, her arms folded beneath her breasts, and walked out in front of the car, the headlights paling her skin. She looked at the spot where they'd put her father, the shells brown from mud where David had washed them, and her expression made me think she could see the shooting, had to wait for it to run its course. I took my pistol from under the seat, got out of the car and glanced over at the track where the three boys had been that morning. A train blew its horn somewhere out of sight. Caitlin knelt and touched the shells with her hand, then stood and inhaled. The wet air was clogged with burnoff from the plants, the shells under my feet as jagged as broken glass.

"You were right," she said. "I shouldn't have come here. It's got nothing to do with Dad." She walked to her side and got in, but for a second I couldn't move for staring at Triche's truck. When I got back in the car, I slid the pistol under the seat and locked our doors.

Caitlin was already smoking again. I watched her lips pull on the thin cigarette, watched her take the smoke deep in her lungs, then slowly blow it back out. She looked at me.

"Last December he kept talking about his and Mother's friends deserting him. He railed on and on, although I know he hadn't called them either. All of a sudden, then, he became introspective, unusual for him. He said lately he'd noticed himself a lot more, said he had conversations with himself and went out for drives in the middle of the night, sometimes slept through whole weekends. He told me he missed Mother and he still loved her, but he'd found that what he missed most was the shape his life used to have. The shape was what he'd liked most about himself." She looked toward the refineries. "I should get back," she said. She drew another puff from her cigarette, then rolled down her window and tossed it out.

"Where are you staying?" I asked.

"At the hospital. Just in case."

"I don't want this to sound wrong, but I have a large house. If you want to get some rest, I'd be glad to have you stay."

She shook her head. "I should stay at the hospital." She glanced at me. "I appreciate it, it's just I need to be there."

I looked out at the drab metal warehouse, at the hard flat lot and the stinking fires in the distance, everything I saw five days a week. I remembered the fear so powerful my legs had disappeared, so powerful that for a moment I'd thought I pissed my pants. It was quiet, and I had to fight the urge to reach over and touch Caitlin, not in a sexual way, just a touch. I cranked the car.

••

"Back off, Miller," David said, pointing his finger at me. "You been riding my ass all morning."

"Pay attention to what you're doing then," I said. He'd just jabbed the forklift through a bundle of PVC. "You make too many expensive mistakes."

David jumped off the forklift and stormed toward the parking lot. Two of the other guys gave me a look that told me I was being an asshole, but when I looked at the shattered plastic impaled on the lift, I turned and walked after David, the stacks of pipe looming on either side of me. I had spent the night in my office, then that morning had Strickland's truck towed to a garage where I knew some guys who would clean it. Now as I walked toward David's back, I saw that Triche's truck was gone, too. I detoured into Alan's office.

"Jesus, you look like hell, Miller," Alan said.

"What happened to Triche's truck?"

"Triche? The shooter? He got it about an hour ago. He must be out on bail." Alan walked over to the coffee pot, poured a cup and handed it to me. "You look like you could use it."

I went to the window and looked out at the parking lot, the sun glaring off the white shells. I took a gulp of coffee, the liquid so hot it scalded my throat. "Goddamnit," I said, after I'd caught my breath. Alan's mouth hung open. I rarely cursed.

"You stay up all night?" he asked. "I hear you're busting everybody's balls again today."

I pressed my eyes, trying to wet them. "Maybe I should've gone home last night."

"I've never seen you so agitated. Is something going on with your ex?"

It took me a second to figure out what he meant by "ex," then another second to push down the queasiness it gave me.

"It's this shooting. I can't get it out of my head."

"Nothing you can do about it." Alan came around to my side. "It is bullshit that bastard being out of jail, though." In the lot, David toed the shells where Strickland had been. Sunshine on the windshield of my car made a fireball.

"You talked to her lately, Miller? Your wife?"

"Why?"

"Just wondering. I know it's not my business."

I shook my head. "Not in a couple of months." I tested my fingertip in the coffee. It was still steaming. Slowly I submerged my finger, burning, until it touched the bottom of the cup. I held it there until it started to numb, then pulled it out and wiped it on my pants. Alan was staring at me. "You got any problem me taking the rest of the day off?" I asked.

"No. Just get some sleep so I don't have another shooting on my hands."

Coming out of the office, the warehouse hit me like steam, summertime elbowing into early April. When I walked up to David, he ignored me. Near his foot was a spot he'd dug out with his boot. I pushed down the urge to say something and motioned to where Strickland had been.

"Think that place'll ever be the same?" I asked.

David shrugged and scooped sweat from his eye socket. "Shit happens," he said.

••

The newspaper listed Triche's address as several miles north of the office in the blue-collar subdivisions not far from mine and Evelyn's first place. The houses became smaller the closer I got to Triche's, the asphalt streets pockmarked and crumbling into the shallow ditches at their sides. For Sale signs lined some of the streets, the white flight that Evelyn and I had been a part of. Triche lived on Sherwood Drive, a street only a car-and-a-half wide and made narrower by the parked vehicles straddling the edges of the road. The yards were worn and balding, rutted by tires and cluttered with scraggly trees and bushes. Two houses from Triche's address I pulled off into the slope of a ditch behind an old Plymouth on cinder blocks.

Triche stood inside the chain-link fence surrounding his yard, hoeing weeds around the clumps of monkey grass that lined his sidewalk. The yellow paint of his low, frame house gleamed in comparison to his neighbors', the ironwork lattices on the porch shone as though freshly scrubbed. Triche used careful strokes as he weeded. A dark patch of sweat stained his shirt between his shoulder blades. When he finished he turned on a water faucet and scrubbed the dirt from the hoe with his thumb and index finger, then leaned the hoe against the house.

At his truck, which sat with its hood up, he shook his head as he ran his hand over the dented fender where Strickland had supposedly hit him. He laid down, reached under the truck and brought out a round plastic pan. Carefully, he carried the pan across the yard to one end of his shallow drainage ditch. The grass was full on the slopes but dead along the bottom to help the water flow. Triche lined up facing the length of the ditch and poured oil in a steady stream down the bald strip. He took meticulous steps, strings of muscle standing from his arms and shoulders, the oil flowing in a black line until he reached his driveway and the pan ran out. He propped the pan against the culvert, wiped his hands on a bandanna and returned to his truck.

My hands went cold on the wheel. I had no idea why I was there watching him, watching this man who had lost control and thrown away everything he'd worked to keep so nice, everything he could depend on. I didn't understand him, didn't understand what exactly could make him do what he'd done, and I wanted to get away from him as quickly as I could. I started my car and drove past him. He looked up, took one step back from the truck and tilted his head, my face setting off an alarm.

I pushed the gas. At the end of the street, I saw him in my rearview mirror, his hands on top of the fence as he watched me go, and that's when something strange happened. I thought of Evelyn, imagined myself as Evelyn, looking back at our house as she left for the last time.

••

Afternoon visiting at the hospital had just ended and people were milling in the hall or straggling from ICU. I checked the smoking section for Caitlin, then sat in one of the plastic chairs to wait for her to come out from her father's room. Near me a woman and man talked about how much better they thought their son was. On the other side of the room a group of people laughed and then collapsed into silence.

After Triche's house I'd driven home and eaten, then tried to take a nap before going back to see Caitlin, but every noise—the thermostat vibrating, the ice maker kicking on, cars passing—had sharpened my attention. Now a calm settled on me. I drifted, dozed, slipped into a dream of a train light bearing down on me, my car stalled on the tracks. I started, saw I was the only one left in the waiting room.

I hurried to the electronic doors of the unit, afraid I'd missed Caitlin, hesitated, then hit the button with my palm and walked in. The oxygen tingled my forehead from the inside out. A short, black-haired nurse met me, her face stern.

"Excuse me," I said. "I was supposed to meet Caitlin Strickland. Her father's in here."

"You're with the family?"

"I'm a friend. I wondered how he was doing."

"I'm very sorry. Mr. Strickland died several hours ago," she said, her tone strictly business.

"He died?" The curtain was drawn across the window to his cubicle, and I had to fight the impulse to go over and check.

"Would you like to sit down for a second?" the nurse asked.

"No, no thank you. His daughter, do you know where she is now? Did she leave a message?"

"I don't believe she did."

I nodded and walked back out. Caitlin had my card. Why hadn't she called me? I rubbed my face. I realized it was ludicrous for me to want that. She didn't know me. I didn't even know her father. Still, I wanted to talk to her, to somebody. Without thinking I went to the phone, intending to call Evelyn. I dropped a quarter in, went to punch a number and froze. I had no idea what her number was. I hadn't called her in five months. Besides, what could I tell her? She didn't know what had happened. She'd think I was crazy for calling, would be angry that I'd never returned her calls and then had called her out of the blue, even if it was to share something like she was always after me to do.

I went to the window and looked across at another section of the hospital, its windows blocked by blinds. Between the sections stretched a space of flat roof covered with rocks. On the rocks lay a single piece of bent metal. I tried to think of someone to call, considered calling Alan just to let him know, then spun and headed for the parking lot.

I got in my car and drove. The odor of Caitlin's cigarettes was heavy and dry but the smell of her lotion still snuck through, reminding me not of her as much as Evelyn. Where was Evelyn right then? At work probably, but I couldn't picture it. I didn't even know where she lived, had tried hard not to know. Before she'd walked out, I told her that we were married, that I loved her, that those were the things that were real, even if I didn't show them like she wanted. She hadn't raised her voice or cried or hit me like she'd done before, hadn't done anything but pick up her bag, her face without emotion, and tell me she'd get the rest when I was at work. And her face, like a wall, like a stranger, like my face I guess, stopped me from even walking outside until I knew she was at the end of the block.

Traffic weaved in and out around me, edged up close behind me, passed so close I could've touched it. I wrenched my hands on the steering wheel. I knew there was something else I could have said, words that would have kept her, even though I still didn't know what they were. And I knew then that I was driving toward Triche's house.

••

It was twilight when I got there. Triche wasn't in his yard, but his truck was. I didn't know why I had come, just that I had to see him, maybe ask him why he'd let himself wreck everything, let himself kill a man and ruin his own life. I started to get out, then pulled the .38 from under the seat, untucked my shirt and hooked the holster onto my belt just in case. At his door I knocked two times. No one answered. I could hear a steady motor running, but there was no noise from inside. I knocked again, loud and hard this time, then looked through the high rectangular window on the door, saw on the wall an amateurish painting of a deer sniffing the wind.

"Yeah?" came Triche's voice from the corner by the carport, surprising me. "You need something?" He had welder's goggles on the top of his head. In his gloved hand, he held a lattice of thin wire. He looked at my car and back to me again, frowning.

"My name's Miller Terrell," I said. "I need to talk to you."

"I'm working around back. The front's locked. People been breaking in around here."

I followed him under the carport, watching the smudges of rust and streaks of black on his tight shoulder muscles. The motor I had heard was his welding machine. He turned it off and tossed his gloves onto a workbench among a pile of bent, burned wire.

"Traps," he said, motioning to a stack of cages. "I sell 'em to trappers down around Dulac. Catch muskrat and nutria in them." He took off his goggles and ran his fingers through his sweaty hair. "I don't want nothing to do with the things myself. All them yellow teeth. Ain't nothing but big rats." We were five feet apart, so close I could smell his sweat. I guessed he knew who I was. "You want to come in?" he asked me.

His kitchen was small and square, close. He put on an undershirt, then sat at a red table shoved against the wall and took off his boots. He crossed his legs one at a time and rubbed his ankles, grimacing as he worked each foot. In his socks he padded over to the sink to wash his hands, a circular fluorescent light buzzing and flickering overhead. The odor of coffee brewed too long bittered the air. Triche squirted dishwashing liquid on his hands and rubbed them together, his back to me.

"I seen you drive by and check me out," he said. He turned as he dried his hands on a towel. "I'm sorry if I messed things up at work for you."

"Messed things up?"

"Talking to you, you know, after the shit. The dude who shot somebody acting like he knows you. I thought maybe it embarrassed you or something. You want a beer? Some coffee?"

The fluorescent light buzzed louder and flickered like a small bolt of lightning. I squinted and blinked, felt a warm pass across my forehead. "Strickland died," I said.

Triche stopped drying his hands. "How you know?"

"I was at the hospital."

He tossed the towel on the counter and leaned there, breathing through his mouth. "Fuck," he said, his voice low. With his fingers he pulled his cheeks downward, then stretched the front of his undershirt with one hand. His face flushed like he was about to cry. "I didn't even know him," he said. "All I'm doing is going to work when he rams into me and takes off like some maniac. I thought the dude was going for a gun." He widened his eyes. "You a friend of his?"

"The first time I saw him was when you shot him. I met his daughter at the hospital."

"I didn't want to hurt nobody, man. Everything happened so fast. You seen him. It looked like him or me." He reached into the refrigerator and brought out a can of beer. "You want one?" he asked.

I stood. "You killed a man. Don't you understand? You killed a man!"

"No shit I killed him. I was there. If I had to do it again I'd kill him again. You understand? You ain't me, man. You wasn't in my shoes when I seen the guy reaching for that piece." He took a long drink and ran his fingers around the rim of the can. "Shit!" he said, and threw the beer against the wall. He walked at me, but when I stepped back he went past. I followed him through the door and stopped, my hand next to the pistol, next to it more because it was something to hold onto than because I was thinking of using it.

In the living room, he wheeled but he didn't move toward me. Instead, he did a frantic dance, flinging his arms in the air and running in place, like a joke. He stopped and covered his face, made a sound like somebody had jumped out and scared him. I stepped back to the door, putting my hand on the pistol.

"What's your name?" he said.

"Miller."

"What do you want, Miller? You going to take me in to the cops?" He laughed. "Fuck you. What do you know, man? Fucking pipe seller." He started walking back and forth across the room, rubbing his hands on his chest. He moved faster and faster until he stopped and held his hands in front of him like he was holding a book. "All I see is his face, hanging there when I popped him, like he couldn't believe it. I see it and I say, 'What is this? I shot this guy.' But there ain't no turn-ing back. It hap-pened. You know what I mean?" He shrugged and shook his head, then dropped onto the vinyl couch. He propped his elbows on his knees and tapped his feet.

I felt sick. Why was I here? Because my life was dam-aged? I hadn't damaged it, had I? I'd tried hard to con-tain things, to keep things working. Not like Triche. He'd thrown it all away because a stranger had dented his truck. I pulled the gun out. I didn't think about it. I couldn't say now why I did it. I pointed it at him. "Hey," I said, and my voice sounded to me like I was waking someone up. His expression didn't change.

"You ain't gonna shoot me," he said, disgusted, and I hated him for talking like he knew me.

"Get up," I said, and took a step forward and to the front of him, holding my arm straight out and closer to him. He smiled and the smile worked its way into laugh-ter and the wild look I'd seen in the parking lot. He stood.

"Shoot me," he said fast, throwing his arms up and feinting at me. I moved back. He laughed. "Big man.

Come on. Put one right here." He stuck out his bony chest and pointed at its center. "Come on. Come on!" He slapped the pistol with the tips of his fingers and leaned toward me, his hands open like he was going to grab me, his face strained and desperate like when he'd come up to look at Strickland. "You got a bone in you? Do it or I'll do you. How 'bout that? Self-defense. You won't even count."

My pulse was all in my fingertip. One squeeze and he would be on the floor dying, waiting to die like he'd made Strickland wait. I'd be there watching, just me and him in his living room, watching him until he was gone, until I was there by myself, carrying it all. I pulled the trigger, slowly, and let the hammer down with my thumb. I lowered the gun.

"That's what I thought," he said. He sat on the couch again and covered his face with his hands.

I turned my hand so that the gun laid in my palm. Then I glanced around the room. On the walls hung primitive paintings of wild turkeys and ducks, the word "Triche" in each corner. There was a recliner and a TV and a coffee table. The wood floor was immaculate. His house was clean and sparse like my house. And for some reason I remembered Evelyn's palms held skyward, as if waiting for me to explain something. She'd been crying, wanting to know why I was so cold, why nothing we did had heat anymore. I had wanted to tell her it did, tell her control wasn't death, but I didn't know how. Later I had tried to write a letter.

"Hey, thanks for dropping by," Triche said. "Don't let the door hit you in the ass."

I put the gun in its holster and unlocked the door. I turned to Triche to say something, but he was staring off, gone to a place where there was nothing left but himself. And I knew that was the same place where I was.

# Hardware Man

I was the highest paid hardware man in Baton Rouge. Seven bucks an hour. Doesn't sound like squat, but in the Red Stick hardware war I was big gun. Five years I worked at Leenks. "Leenks—Your Hardware Connection." Started there a month after Allied Chemical fired me, about a year after I split with my old lady, kind of my second wife. During those first days I snorted coke out back on the loading dock just to get through, but even then I was good. I only sold people what they needed and I showed them how to use it. No bullshit. Eight people worked there when I started. On December 24, 1989, when the hardware superstores forced us to close ney and Patsy Leenk, were left.

We'd planned to have a close-out party, a slow last morning while we helped an Xmas customer or two, but a record arctic front busted half the pipes in town and flooded us with customers, especially dumbasses that didn't know pipe from their own arms. The store was cold as a refrigerator coil and my daddy, who came in town for the party, had on a thick, brown coat lined with fake sheep's wool and jeans that hung loose like his legs were dowel sticks. Earlier Rodney had walked up to me and said, "Shoplifting time, Bob," meaning I could

have anything I really wanted, and every few minutes
Daddy checked out some new feature on the Swiss army
knife I'd salvaged for him. Over in the electrical section
I caught him looking through the magnifying glass at colored lightbulbs, then in the garden tools department he
had the little scissors out clipping his fingernails. That
afternoon me and Daddy were travelling to Galveston
to see my younger brother, Jeb, my first time to see him
since Momma died.

It was almost noon and I had this brunette holding
a piece of PVC pipe, her slender, veiny fingers almost
touching mine as she nodded and smiled, flirting back,
but Patsy and Rodney walked up with these stricken faces
that told me this was our last customer, and I wanted to
hurry and finish the sale before a wad clogged my throat.
I'd just gathered the pipe and tape when the plate-glass
window at the storefront shattered into a million pieces
and a blast slapped me square in the face. Next thing I
was in a tunnel, darkness and flashes and footsteps, and
then I was running toward where Daddy had been standing. The freezing wind hit me like a cluster of tiny nails
and right when I saw Daddy stand, a second explosion
quaked the store so bad fluorescent tubes, cans of spray
paint, and rakes fell into the aisles, clattering and exploding like small-arms fire.

"You all right?" Daddy yelled, coming down the aisle
towards where I was crouched. I nodded back, embarrassed.

"Exxon must've blowed," he said, meaning the

refinery about a mile away. "Cold weather must've messed up the pressure in their pipes. Well, I'll be. Look at that."

In the parking lot, it was snowing black, chunks of insulation floating down from the sky. I glanced around and saw everybody else standing unhurt. "You okay, Daddy?" I asked.

He put his hands up to the sides of his head. "My ears is ringing. That's all."

The five of us crunched over the glass at the front and looked into the distance where fire roiled on the horizon, splotching the cold blue with black smoke.

"Damn, that looks bad," Rodney said. Daddy nodded. While I was in Vietnam, Daddy's plant'd blown an hour before he was supposed to go to work.

On a normal day I'd have already had the brunette's phone number. Now her look told me I was pale green. I excused myself. Heading to the back I tried lighting a cigarette but I couldn't get the match to be still. I wouldn't be walking these aisles anymore. My mother was gone. I didn't know what I'd be doing.

••

Me and Jeb were in the room when Momma died. Her lupus had given her a heart attack and for two weeks she'd fought a coma, finally slipping in four days before she died. Jeb dabbed her lips with a wet cloth, the thing he'd done every time he was in the room. Earlier she'd moved her mouth like she was trying to suckle, but now she struggled just to breathe while I rubbed her feet with lotion and tried to shut out Jeb's telling her that Daddy had gone to the cafeteria with their relatives, his voice sounding like he was talking to a child.

When she went she took one last deep breath like she was ready to rest. Me and Jeb each held a hand and yelled, "Good-bye, Momma. I love you. I'll miss you," so loud a nurse came. Neither of us cried because we were tired, too. Then the room filled up with her and it was like she was hugging me all over at once and I saw red lights danc-ing outside the window, Momma saying good-bye back. I walked over and watched the lights lift into the sky, pause above my apartment across the street, spread out and disappear.

When I turned around, Jeb was sitting in a chair next to the bed still holding her hand. I told him what I'd seen, and he just gave me that "Right, sure" look he's so good at. We had the thermostat low to offset Momma's fever and I shivered, knowing Jeb was going to sit there and hold her hand until the last bit of warmth left her, as if her body, that thing that had let her down, still had some-thing to do with her. I waited in the hall until gurney wheels squeaked toward me and I told Jeb it was time to go.

In the cafeteria Daddy and the others were paying the bill and laughing at some joke, but when we came through the door, Daddy threw his toothpick on the ground and Aunt Autie started crying. Me and Jeb each put an arm around him and walked him out, and in the elevator Jeb told exactly what had happened using that official college teacher's voice he uses when he acts like he's Daddy's daddy. I watched the floor numbers tick higher and pictured Momma's lights zooming past the moon, weaving through asteroids, skimming the rings of Saturn, and heading on towards burning white Alpha Centauri.

•  •

After the explosion, me, Rodney, and Daddy boarded up the broken window. When we finished I hugged Rodney and Patsy and they told me to keep in touch but we all knew we wouldn't. The store made us a family. Without it we weren't. After Rodney and Patsy took off, I got a broom from the loading dock and started sweeping insulation on the parking lot into black mounds. Daddy opened his car door and turned the news channel up loud. *Out of Romania come estimates of twelve thousand dead,* the report said as Daddy watched fire swell the oily cloud over Exxon. The air stank like gasoline and for some reason I thought of the black Martian gas in *War of the Worlds,* a book Jeb had sent me in Nam.

"You put in applications anywhere yet?" Daddy asked.

"The store just closed, Daddy."

"You known about it for a month."

"I'll get unemployment. I'm going to take some time off. I want to go see Teddy."

Teddy's my son. He lives with his mother, my real ex-wife, and her family outside Soso, Mississippi.

American soldiers are playing heavy metal music hoping to drive General Noriega out of hiding in the Vatican compound.

"Who would've thought all the stuff that's happened this year would've happened," I said.

"Hard to believe what all I seen," Daddy said. "The Depression, World War II, communist thugs getting back what they gave. The world's finally turning."

Automatic weapons fire crackled from a live report. I imagined Teddy in fatigues, standing with an M-16 at some checkpoint. I was glad he was only fifteen. "Thank God I could do my part to stem the Red threat," I said.

Daddy twisted the corner of his mouth.

"Lots of men had to fight in wars, Bob. I fought mine."

"Yours wasn't total bullshit politics."

"Every war's politics."

"Not like that one."

"You could've had it worse." Daddy walked next door in front of the Radio Shack where a thirty-foot inflatable snowman stood. He tugged one of the guy wires, wobbling the promo balloon. I wished I hadn't mentioned Nam. Like everything else, the wars we'd been in were something we couldn't share. I'd never been able to tell him what had gone on with me and he'd never been willing to tell me what had gone on with him. He told Jeb about being on Midway when the Japanese fleet passed nearby a second time in 1943 and about being in the first fleet to enter Nagasaki after the bomb, but all he'd ever said to me was, "I was just a Seabee trying not to let my hammer get rusty." When I told Jeb I wished Daddy talked to me like he talked to him, Jeb said, "You blame him for your going to Nam, and he blames you for blaming him. What do you expect?"

I started using a piece of cardboard as a dustpan, and Daddy came back to help. *Record cold temperatures again tonight as the Siberian Express continues to travel through the South.* TV pictures the night before had shown cars sliding on slush in New Orleans and palm trees thrashing in snow.

"Interstate over the Atchafalaya might be froze," Daddy said. "I don't remember it being this cold since right after Winona and me come here."

"Ain't it strange how it's all happening this year?" I said. "The Iron Curtain coming down and the cold front and then that explosion today. I bet Momma's getting a kick out of everything being crazy since she's gone."

Daddy stood and worked his knee like a hinge until it popped, then went off toward the dumpster, carrying the platter of black insulation. I rested my chin on the end of the broom. My hands were numb, the tip of my nose gone. A small explosion rolled like artillery and the sirens seemed like they'd never quit.

••

This was my war: On the flight to Nam, the pilot came on the intercom and told us if we looked out the window to the right we'd see Apollo 13, the moonshot that got crippled, parachuting down. We all crowded over to one side, pressing together and sweating, trying to get our faces close to these little windows, but all we saw was sky and sea. Then the pilot comes on again, real sheepish, and tells us he screwed up, we missed it because he was sitting backwards in the navigator's chair and should have told us to look out the left side.

In Nam I was stationed at Chu Lai. I went out on patrols but mostly I drove freshly wounded in my bus and put people and parts in bags. When I had five days left, this firebase not far from us got overrun. They choppered the bodies, about two hundred Americans, back to this air-conditioned warehouse and laid them out until me and three other guys could go over and bag them. Cambodia was on, so we were busy and didn't get to the warehouse until afternoon. It was dark in there after being in the sun, and quiet except for the AC's hum, so we stopped inside the door. When we flicked a switch, banks of fluorescent lights blinked a couple of times before buzzing on. And there they were. All two hundred of those dead fuckers, their muscles contracted, sitting up in neat rows waiting for us. I turned around and walked back to the CO's office.

"I quit," I said.

••

The ditches next to the interstate were frozen hard as concrete, but the road had thawed. In the median a tractor-trailer rig had crashed, throwing its load of pipes in heaps except for a couple that had jabbed the ground and angled like they were sticking from turrets. The sky shone deep blue. A pale crescent moon ran away from the sun. A daylight moon spooks me because it's something out of place, like the cold weather, like when Halley's Comet drew all the crazies out of hiding and into the store. Jeb thinks I'm full of shit for watching the sky, but what's happening there fucks with people's heads. If the moon can pull the ocean, it can tilt a brain.

"I hear they're opening a new plant down around St. Gabriel," Daddy said.

"Yeah, and they'll be hiring twenty-two-year-olds to be operators."

"You don't know that. You won't get it unless you try."

"I don't want to work in a plant again, Daddy. All those chemicals at Allied made me sick before."

"You should've never lost that job. If you'd learn how to keep your mouth closed."

Coming towards us, headlights shimmered from a convoy of green military vehicles. Following the lead jeep were troop trucks, smaller trucks towing artillery, several armored half-tracks, and a medical truck, regular army stirred up from Fort Polk by Panama.

"Pastor says all this turmoil's the start of the Last Days. 'Revelation,'" Daddy said, watching the last of the convoy. He wiped his nose with a handkerchief. "Maybe you can get on at another hardware."

Years before, when I'd bucked the police department's brass and refused to bury a DWI on a rich asshole friend of the D.A.'s, Daddy'd almost seemed proud. But when they put me on a permanent beat in deserted downtown

B.R. until I quit, Daddy gave me that look that told me I still wasn't gonna turn out right. His words had that look now.

"Could we just drop the job talk?" I said. Daddy turned away and tugged at his ear. "Thank you," I said.

Soon we reached the elevated interstate over the swamp between Baton Rouge and Lafayette. Cypress knees and rotting oil platforms jutted from the water, but the water was frozen white as far as we could see. Around the tree trunks, little ice waves glinted the bright sun like they were chrome.

"You ever seen this frozen, Daddy?"

"Never. I can't recall it ever being froze."

A white egret glided over the road and Daddy watched it as we left it behind.

"Winona woulda loved to seen this," Daddy said. "She always wanted to see a real winter. Look at there."

A bateau with two men in it slowly sawed a path, the boat rising up onto the surface then breaking through. One of the men had on a droopy toboggan cap the color of a roadside cone—a high visibility Santa.

"You know how hard your mother worked to make last Christmas like the old days?" Daddy said. "She told me she wouldn't get to see another one." Daddy kept looking out the side window, the bald spot on the back of his head tanned from working in his yard.

"I think it made her happy," I said.

He nodded. "You know," he said, and tapped a knuckle on the window, "we'll probly never see this again."

••

I tried to get Momma not to do too much her last Christmas, three months before she died, but she wasn't having any of that. She baked pies and made her green-Jell-O, whipped-cream, pecan dish. On Christmas morning, her smile cut through the swollen cortisone skin, her wit sharp in spite of the drugs that sometimes dulled her. After lunch we ate her special dessert, then Daddy and Conlee, Jeb's wife, went for a walk while we sorted through old Christmas photos.

"Look at this one," Teddy said. He held out a photo of me and Jeb wearing jet-pilot helmets, large tin cans strapped to our backs, a big football in Jeb's arms. I was about twelve, Jeb three.

"Steve Canyon," I said.

"Did you always carry that ball?" Teddy asked Jeb.

"Until your dad went to Vietnam. I never would've played basketball if the war hadn't started."

Teddy unhooked my tape measure from my belt. Already he had the beginnings of a moustache, but he also had something I hadn't noticed—Jeb's smirk. I took back the tape.

"You always wear that thing, Dad?" Teddy asked.

"Always," I said. "Protects me from idiots at the store. Whenever somebody gives me a hard time, I stretch this tape out in front of their nose"—I stretched it—"and say, 'I got this much patience left for you,' then press the button." The tape snapped back in. Teddy laughed, but Jeb shook his head and picked up another photo.

"What?" I asked.

"Nothing," Jeb said.

"No, I know that expression. What is it?"

Jeb nudged his glasses up his nose. "Do you get in some customer's face every day?"

"What do you think?"

"I think you talk a lot about telling people off."

"So?"

"I'm just saying. You asked."

"Y'all cool it," Teddy said. He drilled me with a look, then put on the headphones I'd given him. I got up to let myself get level again, but when I stood Jeb started tapping his thumb on his thigh, the smirk painted on his face.

"You got something else to say?" I asked.

"You don't want to hear it."

"I'm listening."

He glanced at Teddy who was nodding to a beat.

"I don't think it's good for Teddy to always hear you talking like you do about work."

"They're funny stories, Jeb."

"No, they're stories about how tough you are."

"Of course, you could do better at my job."

"I could be more diplomatic."

"When's the last time you worked in the real world?"

"I deal with students and colleagues every day. I don't push things in their faces."

"Come sell hardware a week before you start preaching."

"You've still got that cop's attitude, Bob."

"And you know every damn thing about everything, Jeb."

Momma's rasping snore stopped me. She slumped in her recliner, her chin dropped forward near her chest. My eyes met Jeb's. He looked down.

••

"Jeb told me a lady astronaut who lives there is gonna be on the next space shuttle," Daddy said, pointing to a large bayfront house. The houses at that end of Jeb's street, especially the ones on the bay side, were fancy, but the closer we got to Jeb's the smaller they shrunk, the houses on his side looking more like weekend getaway camps, the kind people had at False River and Old River. "Jeb would've got his degree in engineering, he'd be living next to the bay," Daddy said. "That's his there."

He nodded at the last house on the right, a place on stilts with redwood shingles on the sides. A fat Christmas tree blinked behind sliding glass doors, a single-pointed red star on its peak. In the front yard, a plywood alligator with a glowing Rudolph nose lifted Santa in a pirogue. The lot next to Jeb's stood empty, marsh grass standing like broom bristles around an iced-over pond in the lot's center. Jeb greeted us like we'd been having Christmas at his house forever, exactly like I knew he would. He has these tiny round glasses and a cheesy goatee that make him look like Lenin or some other freak. He hugged Daddy, then me.

"Conlee's gone to the store," he said. "Y'all have to put on the snow chains coming over?" he joked.

"Only the swamp's still iced," I said. Daddy was staring across the street at a seawall being built around a house and at the lot next to it filled with huge chunks of concrete. On the side of Jeb's house, a rusty shovel lay on a pile of sand next to a stack of weathered boards. "Nice place," I said.

"The last hurricane washed away everything on that side, but it didn't touch this house," Jeb said. "I got a great deal." He smiled. "It's freezing. Let's go in." He draped his arms over us. "I saw about Exxon on the news. Were you at the store when it blew?"

"Me and Daddy both. Busted the front glass."

Jeb laughed. "The sensational's always chasing you down, isn't it?" he said.

In the living room, with its fireplace and couches, the house seemed bigger than it had outside. Jeb asked if we wanted a beer and while he was gone, I ran my fingers over the spines of Conlee's law books and Jeb's Vietnam books. Jeb's a teacher at a small college and a Vietnam buff. For a while he tried to get me to read some stuff about it, but I told him living it had been plenty for me. Next to the books was a photo of Momma and Daddy on their wedding day. Momma wore a long-sleeved, forties dress suit that hugged her middle and showed off her tall slimness. At her throat were cauliflower ruffles next to a white corsage. Her blond, wavy hair was parted to the side and lifted from her shoulders. She smiled her slightly buck-toothed smile and held Daddy's hand as the camera caught him speaking, shy but happy in his double-breasted suit. I wished I hadn't come.

"I better get the suitcases," Daddy said, standing in front of the TV watching CNN. Me and Jeb told him to sit down.

A gust of wind came from the direction of the bay just as we opened the trunk. Jeb stomped his feet and bent his shoulders. "I can't believe how cold it is," Jeb said. "Last Christmas we were in short sleeves." His face didn't register that mentioning last Christmas made him feel anything. I handed him Daddy's bag.

"What room am I in?" I said.

••

Summer before last, me, Daddy, and Jeb got in a big yelling fight. Jeb was in town to visit and him and Daddy had ganged up on me saying how I needed to get another job and start thinking how I was going to send Teddy to college. What they were saying didn't piss me off as much as the way they said it, talking to me like I was a little kid, especially Jeb. I told them both to fuck off and blew out of the house, thinking I was going to leave, but I leaned against my truck in the wet heat to smoke a cigarette and wind down. Momma came out after me on her walker.

"You shouldn't be walking this far with it this hot,

Momma," I said, but she kept coming, her face set hard in the blue streetlight in the front yard.

"What you think you're doing?" she said. She almost never lost her temper, but I could see her shaking from more than the effort of standing.

"I'm tired of them giving me crap," I said.

"I don't care what you're tired of. This is a family time."

"I'm sorry."

"No you're not. None of you are. I told them, too. All y'all care about are yourselves or else it wouldn't happen. Grown men acting like children. I'm sick of it."

"I'm sick of them."

"Shut up."

She wavered. I grabbed her arms.

"Sit on the swing," I said.

I helped her over, the sweat catching light on her forehead, her body already moist through her clothes. The chains creaked from her weight. She kept her eyes on the ground.

"Momma?"

"I don't understand y'all. We get together once or twice a year and we can't have peace. How long do y'all think I have?" My legs went rubbery. I sat beside her. The night sky was dark and moonless. The radio tower on the road behind the house threw flashes like lightning, showing one thin cloud, pointed like a finger, creeping over.

"Why can't you get along?" she asked.

"Why can't Daddy treat me like he does Jeb? He's never thought I was worth a shit."

"That's not true."

"Nothing I do makes him happy. I volunteered for the goddamn army and all he could say when I came back was get a haircut."

Momma ran one hand across the back of the other, then looked at the dry skin there. I put my arm around her shoulder, but she pushed it off. I laid my hands in my lap. I was sick of getting hurt and of hurting everybody. Every time one of us looked the other in the eye it was some kind of challenge.

"You have so much anger in you, Bob. I don't know why. What did we do?"

"You didn't do it, Momma."

She wiped her hand across her eyes and then across her skirt. She looked at me. Her face was so swollen her cheeks looked like gobs of putty. "Don't you know your daddy loves you?" she said.

She touched my face with her hand, hot with the fever she constantly ran. It was the same way she touched me to wake me after I got back from Nam, even though she knew I might hit her. But I never did hit her. Even asleep, I always knew it was her hand.

••

After dinner Jeb made us some drinks and we sank into their living room. Daddy sat in an armchair glancing at the soundless TV, while Conlee and Jeb played curly toes with each other on the couch. Jeb asked Daddy to tell about coming out on the deck of his ship their first morning in Nagasaki Bay and Daddy rubbed his lips with his fingers a while before he started, then stumbled some telling how the fleet got in at night and how they'd had to stay below deck. Then he pictured it.

"So when we come out on deck we was surprised by it, you know, the whole city tore up as far as we could see. We hadn't seen nothing like it. We really didn't even understand it. Then this old boy who was petty officer points way down on the water and there set this little boat with five Japs in it and they was pointing this tiny old cannon up at us. They wasn't saying anything and we didn't know how to talk to them, so we all just kept looking down at them and them up at us, us with our big boat and them with their little gun. Another old boy says to me, 'I thought we sunk the Yamamoto,' and we all laughed but them Japs just kept on sitting there. Finally, after while they rowed off to another big ship and set there for a long time, then another ship, a battleship that time, all day, nobody messing with them and them never shooting. Along about night they went back to shore and we never seen 'em again. Petty officer said we could all be proud we'd won our first sea battle and he'd see we got the proper medals we deserved."

We all laughed, but I remembered the other story Daddy had told Jeb about his truck ride through Nagasaki, about people sitting on piles of rubble all zoned out, about the shadows of people where there weren't any people, about buildings that looked like they'd been sheared by a giant sickle. I saw the bodies still floating there a week after the bomb and worse I saw the Japs' faces in that boat and Daddy's face looking at them, all of them sharing the most terrible thing that had ever happened, but none of them knowing how to speak to each other.

I wanted to shake the feeling, so I started a story of mine about this kook who came in the hardware store during Halley's Comet wanting to know if we had repellium, a metal he could cover his windows with to keep the comet radiation out. I didn't get very far, though, because Jeb busted in and said, "This isn't one of those stories that ends with you saying, 'Then I told the son of a bitch. . . ,' is it?" Conlee gave him a kick, but he just smiled. Daddy sat there holding his drink with both hands, looking away at people on TV chipping the Berlin Wall while the fire popped and Bing Crosby sang and the room was way too small. I saw the black snow falling and Exxon's flames boiling up and I remembered one day this Chinook chopper passing over, a gigantic net slung under it and filled with dead Vietnamese, their arms and legs sticking out like hair on an insect. The chopper went out over the sea and dumped the net and it splashed and sank into the water and I wanted to yell at Daddy sitting there in Jeb's living room, "How do you live with what you saw?" But Daddy just sat there, paper-skinned and bony, his eyes looking through the TV.

"I need to walk," I said.

"It's freezing out there," Daddy said, and I knew he'd say to Conlee and Jeb how fucked up I was when I was gone. I stepped out into the icy air still buttoning my coat. I lit a cigarette on the go, holding the match in both hands, heard Jeb's voice cracking the cold air, his footsteps hammering to catch me. He grabbed my arm, and I wanted to cock him so hard it'd knock the bullshit out of him, but he grabbed me in a way that told me just to wait.

"Mind if I join you?" he asked.

"Do what you want." I pulled my arm away and we headed off from the houses, the night so still and cold it was like walking inside an ice cube.

"I shouldn't have said that," Jeb said. "It was a joke. I didn't mean to come off like such an asshole."

"Right."

"Everything's just so weird."

"No shit."

He looked me in the eye and smoothed the whiskers on his chin like he was trying to make them grow. I doubted I'd even talk to him if he wasn't my brother.

"Down here," he said. "There's an old pier."

We walked the waterfront road between empty lots and lots with construction until Jeb led me over big jagged slabs of concrete toward the water.

"This used to be a restaurant," he said. "People who stayed during the storm say a wall of water knocked the building off its foundation, then dragged it back out."

The boards groaned when we sat. We hung our legs over the black water and I reached under and broke off an icicle the size of a railroad spike. A sliver of moon sat in the sky. Across the bay refinery fires burned, sending a smoky fog out to hug the water.

"Bad luck moon, isn't it?" Jeb said. "Wasn't less-than-half bad news on guard duty?" I pulled out a roach, not really enough to get stoned, and lit it. We each took a couple of hits. "Two hurricanes and a major oil spill here in the last four years," Jeb said. "I figure this place is due some good luck."

When we finished smoking, Jeb's legs were moving back and forth so fast the wood was shaking. "You're freezing, let's go back," I said.

"No, let's stay. I don't feel like being in yet."

We were quiet again a little while. I wanted to feel about my little brother the way I did when we were close, but what I felt instead were screws tightening in my head.

Jeb ripped up a strip of rotten wood. "I've only seen you once since she died. You didn't come see us last time we visited Dad."

"I was busy."

"No you weren't. You were mad at me. What for?"

"You really asking?" I said.

"Yes."

"Cause you act like you're Daddy's daddy. You act like you can make everything all right."

"I don't do that," he said.

"Fine. You don't then."

Jeb stood and hugged himself. He spat into the water.

"I try to make it easier for Dad," he said. "All I want is to make the hard times go faster."

I stood. "Let's hit it."

He touched my arm. I faced him.

"Come on, Bob, let's talk. Who knows when we'll see each other again?"

"Who knows? Maybe not even next Christmas."

Jeb inhaled slowly and shot the air through his nose just like when he was a kid. He raised his hands. "All right," he said. "I'm judgmental. I'll try harder. I worry about Dad, though. You, too. You're my big brother."

I walked past him, stepped through the concrete and headed toward the houses. He matched my stride, but we didn't speak. Through the fog on the water, I saw a boat's red running lights, heard its horn.

"Give me a cigarette," Jeb said. I lit two and gave him one. He pulled hard and blew the smoke upward the way I'd taught him when he'd asked me how to look tougher as a teenager. He smiled.

"Asshole," I said.

"You know, I get jealous of you and Dad when y'all tell war stories," he said. "Know what I mean?"

"Yeah, you're fucked up."

"No, really."

"You were lucky. You've gotten great rolls," I said.

"I have, but I still envy you. I know it's perverse. You've really lived, though. Your life is big. Sometimes I feel like my life's been cut and dried."

"You just got some sense. Don't wish you didn't."

Ahead, I saw a hulking Martian ship on legs. I stopped, a fist in my throat, then realized it was a water tank strung with lights. I blew into my hands.

"I still dream about Mom almost every night," Jeb said. "The worst are when she's alive and young and then I wake up and she's not. You dream about her?" I nodded. "Tell me."

I flicked my cigarette away and started walking again.

"I had one where I was at a table with all these people," I said. "I kept hearing this piano music that nobody else was hearing, real pretty music. So finally I got up like I was going to the john and went to the room where it was coming from, and it was Momma playing the piano. She winked at me and said, 'This is our secret, okay?'"

Jeb took a deep drag and blew a thin stream of smoke, coughed. "I never told you about my trip home after the funeral," he said. "It was like she was sending all kinds of omens. Like she was saying, 'Look out, things are going to be different.'"

"What kinds of omens?"

"Nothing earth-shattering, it's just that they all happened that night. First, we got a gas can wedged under our car. Then a dog about the size of a wolf—maybe it was a wolf—darted in our way so that I had to swerve

onto the shoulder. And then—this was the clincher—
a blue meteorite fell across the road."

"Really?"

"Really. I'd never even seen a shooting star while I was
driving, much less a blue one. It was beautiful."

Jeb stopped in front of his house and looked up at
the sky, so filled with stars they seemed to be looking at
us from just above the houses. I remembered when I was
in basic training, Jeb had sent me a picture he drew. He
was only ten and he'd crayoned two astronauts, one big
and one small, on the moon. On their space suits he'd
written our names.

Jeb ground his cigarette on the sole of his shoe, making a tiny shower of sparks. He put his hands in his
pock-ets.

"When all that happened to me," he said, "when I saw
that meteorite, I thought of you, Bob. I felt like I was you."

"Sure you did."

At the picture window, Daddy smiled and nodded, listening to Conlee. He pointed over us into the darkness.

"I'm serious," Jeb said. "I felt like you."

I shoved him and laughed. "You never felt that good."

# After the River

A river wants to go straight and that spring the Mississippi wanted to bad, wanted to skip the dogleg that
hooked it down past Baton Rouge and New Orleans and
go right through the Old River Structure Lock to the Gulf
of Mexico. Years, the corps of engineers had been rack-
racking about reinforcing the lock, trying to get their hands
deeper in our pockets, but Cheryl and me didn't believe
the river could really shift, not in our lifetime anyway.
The river was something we took for granted, its sludgy
back and turd current a kind of comfort that dulled us
without us even knowing it. Then record snows covered
Minnesota and Wisconsin and all those other states up
there and spring brought the heaviest-ass rains you ever
saw, pouring like buckets into cups on top of all that
winter melt.

At Baton Rouge chunks of ice floated past, telling
Cheryl and me something was screwy and then Old
Muddy started rising faster than stink on a hot day,
on up creeper and creeper so that from downtown
ships looked like they were riding the levee. Near the
bank where Cheryl worked, water seeped onto River
Road, puddling the asphalt rain and shine. Workers
sandbagged the leaky levee and set up pumps to spit
the water back into the river, a move Cheryl said

seemed to her like drinking more to keep from getting drunk. Word went out to stay off the levee to stop it from sogging down and Cheryl actually saw cops nab some kids and tourists who were checking out the swell. That's when we knew it was serious.

South of Baton Rouge, the corps of engineers opened the Bonnet Carré Spillway to take pressure off New Orleans, but the lily-faced engineers who came on TV said that what with the water volume they anticipated, they weren't real sure what was going to happen. Then the youngest-looking one elbowed up to the mike and blurted he wasn't just worried the river would get through the levee, he was worried the whole river was going to try and jump ship. You can believe that kind of talk didn't set well with Governor Fast Eddie and we didn't see that young engineer on the tube again. Eddie said that the corps must have swallowed some bad flood-water, spewing out panic like they were. He crowed it was more likely the moon would singe his hair than it was New Orleans would flood and said that if it did start to flood he'd personally go to the spillway and summon up Jesus himself to keep New Orleans dry. We'd all heard Eddie talk about Jesus before, Satan too, and nobody took that as much of anything.

At work we goofed about it, me and the old-timers with their flood and plant-explosion stories until after a while I thought maybe we were tempting fate and I'm not even superstitious, much. I'd only been at Neptune Polymers a year and I didn't want any stray river screwing my career security, not right after Cheryl and me had bought a new ski boat and laid down a load on a house. Still, Cheryl and me laughed about the whole thing, smoking a doobie during the news and saying, Please, please, Old Man River, don't swamp our dreamboat, laughing like we hadn't a whole lot lately. See, we'd got married straight out of high school thinking two incomes in one house would just double the fun and keep us for good out of the crummy neighborhoods we'd grown up in downwind of Exxon's farts. We wanted to sprout some kids eventually, but first we needed to get all the stuff we'd always wanted and have the freedom to just pick up and party whenever. And I'm telling you those bon temps had roulered for a while until we sunk in a rut, dragging in from work, scarfing something from Taco Hell, arguing over who didn't pay the Titanium SuperCard bill, night after night drifting through another TV evening, Cheryl barely looking at me and our living room feeling about the size of a locker. It was a thrill then come mid-April and the levee was sweating mud onto River Road.

On TV they showed these high bluffs out around St. Francisville and Cheryl stopped mid-chimichanga to look over at me and smile, remembering our early days in heat and out of control when we'd jumped off one of those cliffs into the toxic current only to wash ashore together wet as otters.

"What if it goes?" Cheryl asked, all ashiver.

"We'll be there," I said.

••

Soon New Orleans started going under for real, their drainage system sputtering down like a roulette wheel, and it didn't take long for serious lawlessness to set in like the best Mardi Gras ever. Fast Eddie called out the National Guard and they showed footage of riflemen in boats like they were patrolling Venice, Italy, or some shit. Cheryl and me had to laugh at that and she stood and pulled me to my feet and waved her arms, leading me through these liquid movements she called the river shifter. Then she said, "Let's party, smarty," even though it was Wednesday night. We plugged some beers in our cooler, rolled a fatty for the ride and threw some clothes in a paper sack just in case we decided to ditch work once we hit the Big Easy. Traffic coming out of the Crescent City was bumper to bumper, but our side flowed fast and free, most of the vehicles filled with people who gave us thumbs up or lifted a drink as they passed. Too bad state troopers had the road over Pontchartrain blocked like some goddamn police state. Still, instead of that sending Cheryl and me into one of our piss-and-moan-and-bite-and-groan arguments over nothing, we just pulled roadside and rehashed the good old days when we used to drink sky labs at Pat O's and stagger down to The Dungeon drunk as legislators. Before we knew it we were shooting beers and hugging tight as a couple of teenagers. When the sun raised his hot round head, he found us flat of our backs, hungover roadkill right there on the shoulder.

Before long we heard about deer herds in the Atchafalaya Swamp climbing onto islands thick as locusts, paw-
ing and biting each other for high ground, and then
they started swimming for boats, banging their hooves
against the hulls and screaming creepy as hell. Hunters
bagged them five at a time with their semi-automatics
and Cheryl wondered why Fast Eddie didn't do something to help the poor things. I just shrugged and said,
"People gotta eat." At the plant Goudeau told about
Hurricane Audrey in '57 washing people out of their
beds in the middle of the night. For what reason he told
us that I don't know. Then he started in on how this was
the start of the last days, Revelations, and the dudes on
horses. Old Barefield cracked wasn't there not supposed
to be a flood but fire this time after Noah, and Goudeau
pointed his finger and said iniquity had to be cleansed
before burned. Barefield smirked and said the Mississippi wasn't much good for cleansing what with all the
crap we'd dumped into it and besides why didn't God
start with New York or Houston if he wanted to do some
real good. Goudeau clucked his tongue and said ques-
tioning God's plan like we were doing was one reason
we'd regret saying and doing what we'd said and done
and even though Goudeau had always been full of it,
for an hour I felt like I had a gutful of brine.

Way south, Morgan City started freaking cause they
were dead on in the path of the new river course. Morgan Cityites wailed how something had to be done to
save their great and important town, talking like the

place wasn't the cesspool of the universe, home to every driftwood piece of oilfield trash and serial killer on his way to do a Gulf Coast tour. In a minute Fast Eddie showed up with a flotilla of priests, blessing the waters like mad and chanting to God to stop the rage of the river. They dumped in so much holy water they themselves probably raised the level a good six inches.

On CNN they were talking about coffins bobbing down the streets of New Orleans and float-by shootings and showed a fleet of NOPD wielding some gunboat diplomacy on a bunch of looters at the River Front Casino. Cheryl said she'd heard rumor of rats streaming out of the sewers in New Orleans and stampeding through the French Quarter, spooking the last tourists sticking it out to get rock-bottom beignet prices. Then Cheryl and me took turns baring our teeth and squealing rodent style as one chased the other, a game Cheryl called Last Texan in Jackson Square.

Next day we went to the state capitol building downtown by the river for a twenty-nine-story bird's-eye view and goddamn if the levee on the west side wasn't completely under and our side looking like a sneeze from a sailor would send it splashing into downtown. We high-fived, bought little state capitol replicas from the gift shop and drove south on River Road, the ditches brimming and water covering the asphalt some places. We climbed the levee and Cheryl took off her shoes exposing her feet, cute little buns with toes, then told me the junior loan officer at work said he'd been in army intelligence and kept yakking about the Armageddon Detour, a federal plan to explode nuclear bombs in certain underground salt domes to let the overflow run into the earth. We figured the guy was jankin' her but then we thought again because not many years before an oil derrick had poked a salt dome and collapsed it and that salt dome had sucked down a whole lake, a truck, a house, and almost a couple of fishermen. That got Cheryl and me goofing, imagining water sucking into the ground, pouring like snakes through these big bomb tunnels until it hit molten rock and let out with these giant steam hisses and big-ass volcanoes. That hot wet talk got us going and we started swapping spit, water squishing out of the sod right there under us on the levee until a swarm of mosquitoes clouded around us like some Bible plague and we had to run hell to highwater back to the car.

••

At work, word came out that folks were humping, even couples whose sex lives had gone belly up a quarter century ago. Old Barefield even let on he'd done his wife in a Mexican restaurant bathroom at the mall. All stripe of weirdness began to break. One guy tore his garage down to build an ark, another sealed his house in shrink wrap, still another strapped pontoons to his motorcycle. Squint Millard had heard about creation of the Pointe Coupée Tube Riders, a surf club set on catching the giant wave down the Atchafalaya when the dam lock collapsed. Solemn engineers came into our control room and drank our coffee while they talked about how maybe the river shifting wasn't bullshit. They said a course change wouldn't dry the river bed but would drop the normal level significantly and stop the flow so that everything south of the shift would be perched by the largest, narrowest, most polluted lake ever imagined. The plant couldn't operate more than a week or so without moving water. Then Goudeau started telling how the 1811 New Madrid earthquake in Missouri made the Mississippi flow backward three days and leap out of its bed a mile and never come back because of the sins of the frontier. Old Barefield told him to shut his trap with his friggin 9-1-1-Holy-Christ-with-a-stick stories and before we knew it we were trying to break them up from a brou-haha and then plant security was in breaking us all up from a brawl. Etienne Simac got the worst of it, a pipe across the noggin, but he didn't seem worried, taking as he was a trip down some mental tributary, sitting there muttering about all this being God's judgement on the state for corruption and godlessness while blood poured from his forehead into his eyes.

We all got sent home for the day and I kidnapped Cheryl from the bank, breaking her into a smile big as August sun. We went for oyster po-boys, drive-through daiquiris, and tattoos of Louisiana that when we held our arms together moved the Mississippi to its new course, then Cheryl ruffled my hair and said why didn't we get home and catch the evening news from the couch. We spooned on the sofa like the old days while some Yan-

kees on a talk show slugged each other because somebody'd been screwing somebody who'd been screwing
somebody who wanted to be screwing everybody and I
was finger-walking along the outside of Cheryl's leg when
Fast Eddie came on live at a Biloxi casino placing a million dollar bet that the Old River Structure would hold
and was much better than the Bonnet Carré Spillway,
which had just washed away, leaving New Orleans looking like water world. The corps was bringing in convoys
of huge dumptrucks filled with boulders to shore up
the end of the Old River Structure, but traffic jams of
people massing to see the big giveway were blocking
the road and there were barely enough troopers and
guardsmen to even direct traffic since now the rioting
and looting was in full revel in Morgan City and some
other soon-to-be-Atlantis towns near the coast. Cheryl
and me locked eyes in a mind meld like we hadn't had
since we'd de-cided to get Miami-sunrise-orange tuxedo
jackets for our wedding groomsmen, toasted our sixty-
four-ounce Gator-Inflator daiquiris and hurled our shoes
into the TV screen, causing a blast that set us to laughing like dental patients forgotten under nitrous masks.

We towed our ski boat out to False River, an elbow
lake that used to be part of the Mississippi, and soon we
were taking turns nude skiing even though the water
was nippy as breams' teeth and a hard rain was falling.
Cheryl slalomed like a madwoman, her bare white self
seeming to be midair every time I looked back, and when
she climbed back in the boat she dropped her ski jacket

and magnetted straight to my lap. "Missed you," she said, and laid a king-size sloppy one right on my lips, then her cool damp body was pressing all against mine and we were twisting and groping to the floor of the boat like teens whose parents have left the house for a half hour. We did the nasty right there in the boat in front of everybody, but everybody was doing it or didn't care. Afterward we sat there in the drench talking about what kind of job opportunities there might be in our backwater town once it really was a backwater town and we both quivered and jiggled a bit considering for real how our comfy lives might really change. Cheryl rubbed her arms worried-like and I remembered how in the old days her and me never worried. Back then we'd just gone with the flow, keeping it spiced however we could, dressing up in animal costumes, ordering anchovy and okra pizzas, skipping work for a day of bat hits and game shows, making love in positions like I was a lawnmower Cheryl was pushing or something. Even so, it'd ended with me up alone, channel surfing and playing spin-the-top with my wedding ring on the arm of my chair while Cheryl dreamed without me.

Where had we gone wrong?

Anyway, I checked Cheryl out there naked in a life jacket and all those other people boating in the buff, wild, and I thought maybe these were the last days. All over the world stuff was going down. People shorting each other cash, fires getting lit nobody knew how, dolphins drowning in nets. Bad business. Like me, what I'd done, fishing here for years, catching more than I needed, letting some die before throwing them back, throwing bottles in the water. And why? I didn't know. I looked at the water around us, gray and choppy, and I thought how I loved the lake and catching fish and taking them home to eat with a whopper plate of hush-puppies and a mound of cole slaw and why would I ever do something to hurt that? Then I looked around at how big that lake was and thought how many fish were still in there and no matter what I'd done there would always be fish in that water and I'd love to catch them. And I thought how when water spilled out everywhere with fish then there would be fish everywhere and new spots for fishing and Cheryl and me could go there in our boat and that would be all right. I jumped up and hugged Cheryl and we linked pinkies and made a pact we weren't going to leave no matter what because we loved our state and its governor and its food.

••

Back at the boat dock we found a wild scene like from The Ten Commandments on the pier, all these people dancing around a bonfire of boat cushions and ice chests. Cheryl and me grabbed a bottle of Wild Turkey and blitzed out of there. On the radio we heard there was boat-to-boat fighting between Aryan State storm troopers and people who got pissed when the Aryans' Grand Duke did an infomercial on how the flooding was the fault of the underclass conspiracy to subvert Anglo-Euro Christian values. All over the radio, announcers were howling about carnage and Cheryl lit an A-Pot-Co-Lipt-Us hooter as we sped back towards Red Stick. Out in yards we saw people in camouflage toting guns and a melee or two at a Piggly Wiggly, but traffic was surprisingly light and I pushed as fast as I could, both Cheryl and me knowing we wanted to be up top the capitol when the big shift came.

Parts of downtown were blockaded because of flooding and people were tooling among the glassy bank buildings in their bateaus and bass boats, but we shoved on until our car stalled three blocks from the capitol grounds where we unhooked our own boat and bee-lined for the observation deck. Atop the levee sat a couple of runaway barges, and a certifiable train of ships was lined up heading south trying to escape to the gulf.

The capitol was wide open with nobody in charge and people were tearing chairs and desks out of the senate chamber while one bald woman in a halter top and shorts stood at the senate president's podium calling for abolition of Robert's rules of order. Cheryl and me hopped on the elevator by ourselves and fell quiet as puddles when we realized we hadn't been anywhere without noise in some time. Cheryl's hair was tied in a bandanna and she kept pinching her lower lip and for a second I saw her exactly like I'd seen her the first night we made love right after the Global Wrestling Confederation's Swamp Spectacular at the Centroplex. I had to lean over and kiss her on the ear.

At the twenty-fourth floor we changed to the smaller elevator, walking around a man in a brown suit on his knees praying, stepped past the ransacked gift shop and stepped out onto the observation deck. People five deep were crammed against the wall looking out at the river, but they weren't struggling and no one was talking loud. About half of them had video cams. We snapped our fingers we didn't have one. The rain had stopped and the sky was a glarey gray and I took Cheryl's hand and eased to a spot where we could see up the river in the direction where the artery was going to be severed.

From way down below us the noise of the city blared, horns blowing and guns shooting and engines revving. On the river, freighters and tankers and barges clogged the water, a convoy twelve ships wide and out-of-sight long, stretching around the bend in both directions, while smoke poured from the plants and refineries all churning at max-plus production. The air burned my eyes and nostrils like skunkweed. We stood for a while, people passing bottles and bags of chips and even joints and nobody being Catholic or Baptist or bastard until a voice said, "It went," and I saw a guy take off his radio headphones. The ships laid on their horns and several tried to make passing maneuvers that rammed them into other ships. Still others tried to veer to the levee and some of the sailors dropped lifeboats, suicide with all those ships in a bottleneck.

Cheryl wrapped her arm around my waist and I put

my arm around her shoulders and squeezed and Cheryl's whole body was trembling, I thought, until she pressed a hand against my chest and hugged me with both arms and I found I was the one that was shaking. There was nothing to do for a while except watch the chaos below and think and I thought of worst-case scenarios, a giant wave washing over the banks, toppling the capitol, taking us with it. Then I thought, What if the river did sweep us away, wash the building right from under us, take us into the river and on out to the gulf? That made my bladder convulse. Then I thought, Wouldn't it be worse not to get to eye this? My legs went jelly and my knees buckled a little, but Cheryl held me steady.

A wave did come, a sizeable one like the river had bucked, one that capsized some ships and sent others over the levee crashing into downtown. But then the wild thing started happening, the river not being the river anymore, its water level dropping like somebody had pulled a plug, the levees on both sides rising up like walls, ships left stranded atop them. I swear even up twenty-nine stories high I could hear guys from the boats yelling, then people on the observation deck began crying and screaming and collapsing. A couple laughed.

Now I know everybody dreams about disaster, imagining nuclear bombs or chemical spills or meteorites hit-ting their house, breaking up the ho-hum with a lit-tle gratuitous weak knee, but there we were, Cheryl and me, watching the river we'd watched our whole lives actually leave us. That sucker went down and stayed down, like Huey Long gut shot, and it was the weirdest buzz Cheryl and me ever had, probably ever will have. Cheryl just looked at me, her face gone nine times pale as a death sheet, and said, "Wow." And, you know, I had to say it back.

••

You can believe things got different fast after that, thousands of people getting the hell out of town and people like me getting laid off work. New Orleans lost its water supply completely and the city went kind of Mad Max until the president of the whole country sent in the serious army and they quieted shit somewhat. All in all, things turned out okay, though, I mean other than a few cities going kaput or being washed away and a few thousand people drowning. Plenty of folks are working on the new levee and ports in the Atchafalaya, and Baton Rouge is one huge gambling town where the river is a putrid lake they run these miniature riverboats up and down piloted by these Mark Twain-looking guys. Soon I got hired back on at Neptune dismantling the unit I'd worked in and for a while after that I ran tour groups describing exactly what it'd been like to be there when the Mississippi changed its mind. Even Goudeau came on my tour once, mostly to show how bitter he was that The End hadn't actually come down on us.

The main thing after the initial excitement, though,

was getting through the posthigh depression, like the biggest hangover in history, everybody shuffling around kind of sullen and pissed knowing they'd already seen the wildest thing they were ever going to see. Cheryl and me got real edgy and then real quiet and finally had a huge blowup over whose idea it'd been to bust the TV screen. The bank took our boat and our house and that caused a lot of the old-style grumbling and touchiness we'd had before the river. For kicks we took some trips to where the Old River Structure Lock and the Bonnet Carré Spillway had been. We even took the ferry ride on the New Mississippi all the way south to where Morgan City is now on the bottom, but we might as well have been looking at the spot where a fish jumped as exciting as that was. Finally, to get out of our funk we splurged on a wide-screen TV and subscribed to the Life-Arts channel's World's Greatest Disasters tape series, which we watched every night, ripped, with the lights off and huddled under a tarpaulin. When the latest tape came out, "The Day the Mississippi Missed," we threw a galoshes party, but most of our friends had already split town.

Luckily, Cheryl and me now have jobs working in the old capitol building, a casino since the capital itself moved to Lafayette where Fast Eddie says it should have been all along. We got a better house cheaper because of everybody moving out and then we got jet skis. Yeah, we still get back in that rut we used to get in, but now when every day seems stagnant and every ripple rocks our marital plank, we just look at each other and relive that day up top the capitol. We hold each other and do the screams and the sound of the boats and run through the house hand in hand, whooshing like a wave, the picture of it in our heads, rushing down the river, washing away the old, and leaving us with something special we saw together. After all, we know not many people can say they were there for something.

I mean really something.